Matthew discovers that he is losing his heart to the new doctor.

Matthew leaned at the same time, looking intently into the trees. Gently and gracefully, the canoe tipped over. It filled with water and scrunched against the gravely bottom while they spilled face forward into the deep pool.

They came up laughing and close together until their safety vests bumped against each other, sending them spinning apart. Instinctively, Matthew reached out and caught Emily by the shoulders to keep her close. He found himself wishing they hadn't been so safety conscious as to wear vests. He would have loved to hold her and feel the water making a soft world of their own around them.

He wanted to kiss her. He watched her blink her eyes against the water that engulfed her when she went face down before her vest righted her. He wanted to kiss the drops of water off.

Did she want that too? Her laughing face wasn't saying yes or no, though she must be reading the longing in his eyes. He leaned toward her and she didn't pull away. Her inviting lips were soft and. . .were they waiting?

MARY LOUISE COLLN has enjoyed raising five children while pursuing a career in nursing and writing. She had short stories, articles, and poetry published before her first **Heartsong Presents**, *Mountain House*, was published. This is her second novel.

Books by Mary Louise Colln

HEARTSONG PRESENTS
HP26—Mountain House

A Place for Love

Mary Louise Colln

Heartsong Presents

For the little ones,
Colln, Lindsey, and Marshall.

A note from the Author:
I love to hear from my readers! You may write to me at
the following address: **Mary Louise Colln**
Author Relations
P.O. Box 719
Uhrichsville, OH 44683

ISBN 1-55748-766-9

A PLACE FOR LOVE

Cover illustration by Kay Salem.

PRINTED IN THE U.S.A.

one

"This," said Marcia Cook in her best head nurse voice, "is for our favorite resident of all time. But don't anyone dare tell the next doctor who transfers in."

The laughing group of nurses, orderlies, and clerks gathered in the head nurse's office of Ward 4C promised that they would never tell. Emily Richards, touched by the unusual surprise farewell on the last day of her residency, accepted a gaily wrapped box from Marcia and removed the latest in electronic stethoscopes. She was delighted with the gift and let her happiness show.

"You must realize that a doctor going into a new practice couldn't afford such luxury," she told them.

"We realize that once you get into the wilds of south Arkansas, you won't even be able to find anything beyond glass thermometers," Marcia teased. "In this town called . . .what is that name again?"

"Sawtown." Emily pretended solemnity, running her fingers through her short brown hair. "And it's really a thriving metropolis. It's just hidden away so no one realizes its immense size."

"It sure is hidden away," one of the nurses agreed. "I remember driving by there once and seeing the sign. You have to go off the highway just to get to it."

Marcia sighed. "I know it's no use trying to point out

what a lucrative practice you could set up right here in St. Louis. You could get on the staff here so quick."

Emily shook her head. "I promised them at least two years and if I hadn't. . ."

"I know. You'd go off into the wilds of Africa with Dr. Page instead of the wilds of south Arkansas. The best ones seem to go. . ." She let the sentence trail off and there was a short silence. She broke it by turning toward her desk, which had been changed by a snow white tablecloth and someone's crystal punch bowl into a semi-elegant serving table.

"Well, now, let's sample that cake. I've been walking by it all morning and resisting temptation. You cut, Dr. Richards." She handed Emily a glass of punch and a knife at the same time.

Emily looked at the friendly faces gathered about her, then at the huge home-baked layer cake in front of her.

"All right," she said, in mock dismay, "but, remember, I'm family practice, not a surgeon. Don't expect perfect slices."

She had just passed the cake around when Lorene, the nurse who was watching the patients while they ate, stuck her head in the door of the office.

"Barry's back," she said, her voice tight with stress. "It looks bad."

Plates of uneaten cake and cups of punch were left helter-skelter on the desk as the group made an instant switch back to professional workers. Each of them hurried out to perform some necessary part of caring for the new patient.

Emily stood at the desk for a moment. "God," she asked,

"did he have to come back on my last day? Tomorrow I'll be gone. I could believe that he beat this thing."

In her mind, she pictured five-year-old Barry Green as she had last seen him in Kids Cancer Clinic. The pale little boy's blood count had been too low to continue his chemotherapy for leukemia.

Even though he was no longer her patient, she followed the nurses down the hall to Room 454, where the bed was surrounded by caring professionals. Already a nurse was drawing a small amount of blood for immediate laboratory tests and to prepare blood transfusions. Another nurse prepared intravenous fluids.

Barry looked much too submissive for a five-year-old. It was the patience of someone who had suffered for a lifetime. His mother stood away from the bed, looking as lifeless as Barry.

Dr. Joyce Blake, the new resident who shared a tiny apartment with Emily, was in the room directing the procedures. She looked up briefly and Emily gave her a friendly nod but didn't interrupt. Joyce was a competent doctor and would call a staff doctor for advice if she felt she needed it.

Emily moved to Peggy Green's side. "Why don't we go out to the atrium, while they work?" she said in a low tone, slipping her arm about Peggy's shoulders.

With a look of mute thanks, Peggy stumbled out, leaning heavily on Emily's shorter body. Peggy Green was a strong person, but the last few months had seriously stressed both her strength and her faith.

The late May afternoon sunshine flooded through the windowed walls of the atrium, making the banks of plants seem like an outdoor garden. Emily led Peggy to comfortable seats near the plants.

"Barry always liked this room," Peggy said, looking around.

"Yes, he did." Emily wanted to assure her that he would come out here again, but knew that she shouldn't instill a hope that might not be realized.

"Barry liked plants. We liked to go out to Forest Park in the spring. He liked the animals, too." Peggy continued to talk about what she called "the days before." Before Barry's father had been killed in an auto accident. Before Barry had leukemia. Emily listened, making no attempt to bring her back to the present or guide her memories.

"Dr. Richards, sometimes I don't trust God much." It was a sudden, bald statement.

Emily said a silent prayer for guidance, then simply continued listening as Peggy stumbled her way through her pain and anger, back to a confession of her deep need for God that Emily knew would lead again to trust. They talked quietly for more than an hour of other things, neutral things that seemed to help Peggy.

Emily saw Joyce and the hospital chaplain coming down the hall and held her breath. But they were smiling.

"Barry's improved, Mrs. Green," Dr. Joyce Blake said. "We still have blood transfusions going, but you can see him now. He's asking for you."

"Oh, thank You, God," Peggy breathed, and Emily squeezed her hand. She said a quick good-bye and sent Peggy off with the chaplain while Joyce went on to other patients.

At the doorway of the atrium, Peggy turned to her. "Oh, Dr. Richards, good wishes for your new life in Arkansas. If they aren't good to you, come back. Barry and I will be glad to see you."

Emily laughed and waved. She could leave hoping that Barry would beat his leukemia. She added her whispered "thank You" to Peggy's.

Tomorrow she would be on her way to her new life. Feeling nostalgic as she walked down the hall of 4C for the last time, she stepped into 425 for a quick good-bye to Sonny Phelps and his parents. Sonny was going home, hopeful of a cure, and the shine on his parents' face reflected their joy.

Feeling their happiness inside herself, Emily left the ward. She hurried out of the hospital and headed for her apartment, just off the hospital grounds, still feeling nostalgic and thinking now with pleasure of the honor and affection the staff of 4C had shown her.

She knew that in spite of their half serious attempts to get her to stay in St. Louis, they respected her for her refusal. They knew that the people of Sawtown, a small lumbering community, had helped pay her medical school expenses in return for her promise to practice there for at least two years. Not one of the people gathered around her on her last day in residency would want her to go back on her word.

But someone did want her to change her priorities, Emily admitted ruefully to herself. And emotionally she agreed with him. But she wasn't going to let those people down who counted on her.

The phone was ringing as she unlocked her door. She slammed her purse to the floor and raced toward it, then slowed down. It wasn't going to be the hospital calling. Not ever anymore. Feeling more than a little saddened by the reflection, she lifted the receiver.

"Emily." The familiarly hurried voice on the other end was welcome. "Can you meet me at McGregor's? I think I have time to eat if there's no emergency."

"Of course, Ryan. I'll wait at the usual table."

McGregor's was a no nonsense, no theme restaurant where the emphasis was on serving good food quickly to the medical people who were tired of hospital cafeteria lines. Sitting in their favorite table in the back of the restaurant, Emily watched Dr. Ryan Page thread his way past the mostly empty tables toward her.

He could have been cast by a Hollywood director as the ultimate good doctor. Tall and slender, he wore his dark hair in a classic, swept back style that sometimes let a tress slip down over his blue eyes. Emily had been working with him over the past two years. She knew that the mind behind those eyes was razor sharp.

He could step into a big paying practice here just on the strength of his looks, she thought as he caught her eye and smiled. Then she returned to the problem that had concerned her for several months. *But if he's committed to medical mission by his church and I'm committed to Sawtown, what does the future hold? And do I really love him or the idea of medical mission?*

As he moved through the restaurant toward her, Ryan kept his eyes on Emily the way he would have watched a precious pearl . *I've loved this small woman with her big brown eyes for two years,* he thought to himself. *And now I have to let her go to those people in that little town she won't leave. And I can't push her to go back on her promise and go to Africa with me, or even say she loves me, when she's torn between me and Sawtown. She wouldn't be the honest Emily I love if she did. I'll know she loves me when she comes to me. And the years will be full between now and then.*"

"How does it really feel to be through with residency?" He pulled out a chair with his usual quick motions and sat down opposite Emily. "I want to anticipate my own release from bondage five days hence."

Emily spread her arms. "I made it. I made it. Thank You, God. But you'll soon know for yourself."

He sobered. "Then we start waiting for you to finish your time in Sawtown, Arkansas, so we can begin our lives together."

Emily didn't answer immediately. Ryan had been begging her for several months to wear his ring, but she had put him off.

"That's two years, Ryan," she reminded him gently. "And you'll be in Africa. Your world is going to be so satisfying. You know how much I wish I could go with you, but I can't break my promise and I won't tie you to me till I can join you."

Ryan touched her hand. "Let's not talk about it now. I really respect you for keeping your promise in spite of the fact that I want you to break it and go with me. Are you all packed?"

"I'll finish tonight."

"I wish I could be with you this evening, but," he grimaced and stood up as his beeper went off, "you know how it is."

Emily laughed, a low bubbling sound that made two people at the next table look over and smile. "I haven't been away from the hospital so long that I can't remember how it is," she teased.

"Emily. . ." He leaned on the table, scanning her face intently, almost as if he were memorizing it.

"Ryan, we agreed no sad good-byes. Write to me when you get to your station. You know where I'll be."

This time he groaned. "How could I forget old Sawtown? And I know where I'll want you to be."

"Don't forget I'll want all the details of your life in the field. Everything that will help me when I can come."

His beeper exploded with the stressed voice of a nurse asking for an immediate answer; he kissed Emily quickly on the forehead and hurried off. She knew he would call her several times before he left for Africa, but somehow she'd keep the calls from becoming emotional.

How typical, she thought, that Ryan had not been able to share a last meal with her. She knew that he'd swallow a stale sandwich sometime during the evening.

Actually, she admitted to herself, she was relieved that their last good-bye was too hurried to be wrenchingly sad. They had already spent too many evenings lamenting the years that must pass before they could be together.

She finished her own meal leisurely and ordered a piece of pie, not just because she wanted it, but because suddenly she wanted to savor having the time to eat it. But, she reflected with a smile, the years of little time to eat or sleep had kept her short body slender so she could easily afford the calories.

She walked back to her apartment to start packing. and was standing gazing at the stack of clothes on her bed, waiting to be packed, when Joyce rushed in.

"Oh, Emily, I wish I could spend your last evening with you, but I promised Mom and Dad that I'd appear at their party. You sure you won't go with me?"

"Thanks, but I need to get an early start tomorrow. Tell your folks hi and good-bye for me."

Joyce made a little face at herself in Emily's mirror, then reached up to smooth a tress of her dark hair. "I wouldn't go myself if I hadn't promised. You know, Emily, it all seems so out of touch with the world after something like this afternoon. After Barry. More and more I want to get away and do what you're doing. What Ryan's doing. Not what my dad wants me to do."

"Your dad is a good surgeon, Joyce."

"He is and his patients are willing to pay well for it. He's still pushing me to change my residency from family practice to surgery and go in with him. Well, I'm resisting. . .so far. I want you to know, since you're leaving tomorrow, that I'm more than seriously thinking of coming to Arkansas with you when I finish here next year. I've had money and social life. Now I want a change."

Emily hugged her quickly. Joyce knew that if she chose to come to Sawtown, Emily would feel free to go to Ryan in Africa after her two year commitment was up.

"I hope you'll continue to want it. We'll plan for you to come down to visit after I get my feet on the ground."

"Good. I'll be looking forward to it." Joyce glanced at the expensive watch on her arm and hurried into her room to change. She came back dressed in a sleek black gown that perfectly fit her slender, long-legged body, and that Emily thought probably cost more than her own entire wardrobe. Emily remembered asking her once why she was willing to share an apartment that was within Emily's financial range.

"Your company," Joyce had answered.

Now she hugged Emily in a rush of emotion that Emily felt she was deliberately holding in check by pretending to be in more of a hurry than she actually was. "I'm on duty early tomorrow so, Emily, till I come for that visit. . ."

"I'll write you and send pictures of the clinic Sawtown has built for me. . .and for you."

Flashing her attractive smile through something near to tears, Joyce ran out.

Emily continued packing for an early morning start to Arkansas. "Tomorrow." The word ran through her mind again, half happy, half sad. "Tomorrow I start a new life."

two

Sawtown. Somebody with a wry sense of humor had named the town for its only industry. Emily's car glided more and more often into the shadow of the great walnut and pines on the narrow two-lane road.

She thought of the ugly expanses of clear cut hills farther back where there were only rutted lumber roads. And especially of the hillside where her father had died under a giant maverick tree that had fallen the wrong way—a tree that she had never wanted to see, though she had been told that it was left where it fell. It was the only time she knew of that Morgan Lumber put sentiment before profit.

She entered a particularly shaded patch and smiled to herself, feeling the sudden difference in temperature from the warm day.

This feeling of drifting into a tunnel of trees that met above her head always turned her into a little girl again, playing in the edge of the dense forest in back of her house— and brought back her love for the forest and her resentment of those men who cut it down and allowed her father to die under one of their cuttings.

She wasn't far from home now. Sawtown was just ahead and a few miles out from there her mother would be waiting with a hot meal. Emily felt her foot pressing just a little bit harder on the accelerator as she rounded a gentle curve.

She hit the brakes with a screech. A man was standing almost in the road, waving her down.

Emily's first thought was to swing around him and continue on. The very dimness that she had been enjoying just a moment earlier made him seem more dangerous. But this was Sawtown, Arkansas, where people still trusted and helped each other.

She slowed to a crawl as she realized that the man held a crying child in his arms. A second look told her that the child seemed to have blood on her clothes. Still feeling apprehensive, she pulled toward the edge of the road and stopped.

One handed, the man jerked the door open and tumbled in. Emily watched him jackknife his legs and bend his shoulders to get himself and the child into her small car. Under her immediate concern for the child, she had an eerie feeling that the space inside her car had crumpled and she was much too close to this stranger.

"She's been cut," he said curtly. "You'll have to go back to the highway and take us to Clifton. We've got a new clinic in Sawtown, but the new doc isn't here yet."

"Let me see." Emily reached over to the whimpering child, then let her hand drop to the steering wheel as she saw that the arm had a neat pressure bandage on it.

"I told you," he sounded irritated, as though he was used to having his orders carried out immediately, "you've got to take us to Clifton. It needs stitches and Kate can't do it."

Suddenly the little girl broke into sobs. The man cuddled her tenderly. "It's all right, honey. We'll call your mom from Clifton."

Emily looked them over carefully. She guessed the child to be about eight. She had dirt and leaves as well as blood on her shorts and shirt. Her face and thin legs were smeared, yet under the blood and dirt, she looked reasonably healthy to Emily's trained eye.

Still, she suspected child abuse. Perhaps this man and his daughter were living somewhere in a shack back in the woods. Sometimes whole families did live deep in the woods in tumble-down houses or even tents.

The man certainly didn't look like someone who expected to be instantly obeyed. He had some of the child's blood smeared on his heavy work jeans and wool shirt, his high-cut boots were muddy, his dark hair needed cutting, and he obviously hadn't shaved for several days. Yet there was something about his face—the line of his jaw and an intensity in his dark eyes—that spoke of authority. Emily wasn't sure if she was attracted or repelled by him. But if he had committed child abuse, she was ready to fight him.

She steered the car into the road and forward toward Sawtown.

"I told you. . ." He sounded angry.

Emily looked straight ahead. "I'm the new doc," she said. "We'll go to the clinic." She didn't look to see what effect her announcement had on him.

"You. . ." Emily could feel him studying her face. "Nobody told me the new doc was barely out of her teens."

"Why should they?" Emily always reacted with anger that even in the 1990s she sometimes ran into prejudice for her sex and embarrassingly youthful looks. And she suspected that even if he wasn't saying it, he was thinking about her being a woman.

"Hey, I'm not putting you down. I'm just surprised no one mentioned it."

"Everyone in town knows who I am and what I look like. They probably just didn't think that there would be someone who didn't, no matter how seldom you get into town."

She glanced again at his whiskered face. He seemed to be making a big point of shifting the child in his arms to make her more comfortable. Emily was irritated at the thought that he almost looked like he was trying to hide a smile.

She drove into town. Most of Sawtown was huddled in an elongated rectangle on both sides of the county road. The business buildings, which were also mostly rectangular, housed only the essentials: grocery store, gas station, and the familiar Blue Bird Cafe. Private homes were tucked in among them and all blended together into a timeworn, but pleasing whole. Emily noticed that a couple of antique stores had been opened in unused buildings. Tourism was beginning to penetrate even to Sawtown.

The clinic had been built just off Main on one of the few side streets. As she pulled into the parking lot, she noticed one of the other town changes that her mother had told her about. A short distance beyond the clinic, with its huge parking lot adjoining the clinic's own lot, was a no nonsense looking square building with a sign SAWTOWN FURNITURE across the front.

The new factory was supposed to put Sawtown on the

map and give it a little more boom to its economy. Curiosity caused her to look again at the grounds. She saw, with approval, that several large trees had been left beside the building and picnic tables were set up in a parklike area. She could even see clusters of flowers here and there.

Without waiting to help him get out with the child, Emily strode into the clinic. She admitted to herself that she wanted to make this unsettling man realize that she belonged here. She hoped the equipment for stitching the child's wound had been delivered, or she might have to eat a little crow and take them to Clifton.

Halfway to the clinic building, she realized that she hadn't been given a key yet, and that there was a good possibility that it would be locked and no one there. To her relief, the door opened easily and she stepped into a brightly lit waiting room. It was empty except for several big boxes stacked about the floor and on top of the low counter that separated the reception desk from the rest of the room.

Emily held the door for the other two, then hurried through the waiting room and down the hall, knowing that he was following her without being asked and wishing that she were taller and more imposing.

She heard someone moving about one of the treatment rooms and turned in. It was a mess. Boxes were stacked about the walls and strewn about the floor as if an angry child had thrown them in a tantrum. Some were opened, some still closed. Piles of delivery bills and inventories were scattered across the black plastic of the uncovered treatment table. Doors of the cabinets that lined the walls were open haphazardly and the long counter tops were piled deep in supplies. Yet over it all there was a look of planned control.

Kate Donagan, dressed in jeans and tee shirt instead of her white nurse uniform, looked up from the stacks of boxes she was emptying into some open shelves, her eyes widening in surprise.

"Dr. Richards," she said. "I wasn't expecting you today."

Emily let her own eyes show the pleasure she felt at seeing Kate in charge of her clinic. The pleasant face framed by blunt-cut blonde hair was one she had been familiar with since being a few years behind her in school, and she knew Kate's reputation as a nurse.

"I wasn't expecting to come in today," she said, her experienced eye noticing that there were more supplies than she had dared hope to have. "But I picked up a bum and an injured child on the road. We may have a case of child abuse here. Do we have sutures and instruments? I haven't looked at the wound yet, but she may need stitches. Anyway, he's bringing her in now."

Even as she spoke, Emily wondered why she was taking this strange man's judgment that the wound would need stitches.

Kate's calm answer showed her unflappable competence. "I've set up suture trays we can sterilize and reuse to save money, but I don't have them sterilized yet. We have some disposable sets that I ordered for emergencies. I guess this is one now."

Kate stopped talking abruptly as the man carried the child in and stood looking for a place to put her down. Her face paled and tensed.

"Oh, no," she whispered. "Julie!" she cried. "Julie, what happened to you?"

"She'll be all right, Kate." The man's voice sounded quiet and comforting now. Kate seemed to recognize him.

The child started to cry again and Kate pulled her into her arms, dirt, blood, and all. Emily stood looking at them in bewilderment. What was going on? Kate had lost all semblance of being a nurse. All the calm sureness Emily had been admiring was shattered. She looked frantic.

"Baby, what happened?" She held the trembling child close. "Where did you get her, Matthew?"

"She was lost in the forest, not too far from the road. I haven't questioned her, Kate. Maybe she's not ready to be questioned yet. Let's get her taken care of first."

Kate seemed to suddenly come back to life. "Oh, I'm sorry, Dr. Richards. This is Julie. My daughter. I'll put her on the table and get the suture set."

"Never mind, Kate. There's no need to leave her. And no room on the table. Just point me toward the suture set."

While Emily followed her pointing finger to the correct box on the floor and set the suture tray up on the shining steel instrument tray, Kate sat down with Julie and carefully removed the bandage. The wound was short but fairly deep and starting to bleed again.

It almost looked like the stab wounds Emily had seen in the emergency room in St. Louis, but not nearly so deep. Like someone had taken a quick jab. But, since Julie had been in the woods, it was more likely she had fallen on some old tool left by the lumber workers. Emily reminded herself to ask Kate about her tetanus immunization as soon as she settled down.

All the time that Emily was preparing to treat the wound and saying the small prayer that was routine any time she treated someone, that she would do the right thing and do it well, questions were shooting through the back of her mind.

Her mom had told her that Kate was engaged. Was it to this man? She shot a sharp glance at Kate. Was she giving Julie an abusive stepfather?

She cleaned the wound and deadened the skin around it. Julie, who had cried at sight of her mother, was strangely quiet now. As she worked, Emily was acutely aware of the intense concentration of the man Kate had called Matthew. Almost, she thought, as if he were judging her capabilities.

The thought angered her and she glanced at him sharply, irritated that he knew who she was and she didn't know him. She was tempted to order him out but since Kate seemed comforted by his presence, she decided not to force the issue.

As she finished and put a bandage on the arm, he smiled for the first time since she'd picked him up from the side of the road.

"Good job, Doc." He held out his hand. She pretended to be too busy stripping off her gloves to see it. She wasn't going to accept his judgment on her work.

"Oh," Kate said, in apology. "Dr. Richards, this is Matthew Barnes."

Emily nodded coolly.

"Now, Julie," Kate said quietly, "tell us what happened. Why were you in the woods? Did Bessie give you permission to go?"

"I didn't go, Mommy." Julie started crying again and hid her face against her mother's shoulder. "Daddy took me."

"Julie. You know your father is dead."

"He's not, Mommy. He's not. He came into the yard and said I had to go with him and then he cut me. He said it was to make you know that you can't marry anyone else because he isn't dead. He said he'd cut me worse if you did. Mommy, he told me to tell you." Julie looked intently at Kate, as though begging her mother to believe her.

Kate's face stiffened and turned even whiter, her lips trembling. For a minute she looked as though she might faint. Emily quickly went to her side. "Kate. Are you going to be all right?"

"I. . .Jules can't be back. Jules has to. . ."

She stopped. Emily knew that the words she didn't say were "be dead."

"Kate, you know you have to tell Ben," Matthew Barnes said.

Kate nodded but she didn't move, and Julie was totally relaxed against her shoulder, now that she seemed to realize that her mother believed her. Matthew went out to another room and Emily heard him speaking into a phone. She moved to Kate. "Are you all right now, Kate?"

Kate seemed to pull herself from somewhere far away. "I. . .we'll be all right, Dr. Richards. Thanks for bringing them in and," she tried to laugh, as she added, "starting your work early. You need to go on home now. I know how anxious your mother is to see you. She even took the day off from the Blue Bird to cook for your first evening home."

"You sure you won't need me?"

"No. Matthew will stay till Ben comes."

Emily remembered that Ben MacGowan held the somewhat superfluous title of police chief, since the only other policeman on the staff was Dave Willis, and he was part time. Not much happened to stir things up in Sawtown. Emily was sure he would come right over.

"Then I will go see what Mom has cooked up. I'll check out Julie's arm tomorrow. And, Kate, we've known each other all my life and we're going to be working closely together. Let's not be too formal. O.K.?"

This time Kate did manage a smile. "I've been practicing saying Dr. Richards for months now, so you have to let me use your title sometimes. But whichever I call you, let me tell you now, Emily, I'm glad that you're here."

Emily gave her a quick hug and hurried out, somehow wanting to be gone before the man called Matthew got off the phone. She figured he must be the one Emily was engaged to or he wouldn't have stayed with them so long.

As she drove out of town toward the small house where she grew up, she tried to put the whole thing out of her mind and think about what that great cook, Mom, had for her first dinner home. A stray thought drifted through her mind. How did Kate know that her mother took the day off from the cafe? *Well,* she thought, pulling into the driveway, *who did anything in Sawtown that everyone didn't know about?*

three

"I wonder if any other house in my lifetime will be able to give me that feeling that this house does," Emily asked herself. "Home, that's the feeling. Every time I come for a visit, it's just the same. That same small, neat white house with the patterned tin roof that sounds musical notes when it rains, and the thick forest so solidly in back of it."

She sat and looked into the forest for a minute, remembering how she used to try to look into its depths when she was a small child, knowing that her father had died somewhere in there. She had sometimes thought that if she tried hard enough she could make him walk out of it again as she had a dim memory of him doing. Then he'd pick her up in his strong arms and hold her high in the air.

When her mother found out what she was thinking, she explained again that Daddy was in heaven, not in the forest, and slowly Emily had learned to think of him there.

Her days alone with her mother in the house had been happy ones. It was only later, after she grew up, that she realized how hard her mother had worked to feed and clothe them and keep that loved roof over their heads and the slavering wolf from that pretty red front door.

She brought herself back to the present. She was anxious to see her mother and, she admitted, see what was cooking. She was happily hungry.

Caroline Richards met her at the front door, arms wide. "Emily, Emily, I can't believe it. You're finally home for good."

Emily returned her hug enthusiastically, enjoying the comfort of her mother's slightly plump body in her arms. Her happiness was only marred a bit by the knowledge that, though she had, almost casually, mentioned her desire to go into the mission field with Ryan, she hadn't yet told her mother that she would only stay in Sawtown the required two years.

"Mmm." She drew in a deep breath. "Something smells heavenly. What has the best cook in Sawtown fixed for tonight?"

"Come see. It's ready."

"Just let me put my luggage in my room. I'll unpack later."

"Oh, I've switched rooms with you. You need to be closer to the front door in case you have to leave at night. And I've always thought it might be nice and quiet in the back bedroom. I sleep in there sometimes when you're gone. The swoosh of the wind in the tops of those big trees and the little noises of animals are good company when I'm alone."

"I know." Emily smiled at the memory of lying beside the open window on summer nights hearing the soft call of a whippoorwill or the delicious shiver of a screech owl back in the woods. "But, Mom, are you sure? The front room was your room with Daddy."

"Of course I'm sure. I loved your daddy with all my heart, but he's been gone a long time and I learned years ago that I couldn't live just in memories. And don't worry. You can hear outside things in the front bedroom, too. Oh, I found a bargain in a desk for you. It's in there. And a phone. You're all set, Dr. Richards."

Emily laughed and hugged her mom again before she ran out to get her luggage out of the car.

The room was larger even than Caroline Richard's living room. The desk was big, old-fashioned, with rows of drawers down each side. A comfortable looking arm chair stood in front of it. The dresser and bed with its hand carved headboard and a cushioned rocker were her old stuff. She wondered briefly who had helped her mother move it all.

It looked so achingly familiar and loved that for a minute Emily felt more like a child than a grown-up woman with the letters MD after her name. She gave her slender wooden rocker a loving pat and set her suitcases in the exact center of the red-faded-to-rose, old Oriental rug that her mother had found in some garage sale when she was ten years old. Then she hurried out to the kitchen.

While she was putting her luggage in the room, Caroline had been busy carrying food to her antique dining table. When fully opened, the table was almost as large as the tiny dining room but, except when there was company, Caroline kept it folded to a small area beside double windows looking out into the trees. They sat down to a simple but delicious meal of pot roast with vegetables and huge, fluffy biscuits.

"Emily, this is a day we've worked, hoped, and prayed for. Let's give thanks to the Lord for it."

They bowed their heads while Caroline spoke with God

as though He were in the room with them. Then Emily dug in, enjoying every bite.

"I expected you earlier," Caroline said. "Did you have a problem?"

"Well, sort of a medical problem, sort of a mystery." She told her mother what had happened.

Caroline shook her head. Emily noticed that there were a few more silvery sparkles mixed into her hair, hair much the color of her own but worn in a longer style.

"Jules Donagan is back? I don't believe it. Someone is pretending to be him. God wouldn't let this happen to Kate just when she's about to finally find happiness. Anyway, how could Julie know it was him? She couldn't possible remember him. She was just a baby when he disappeared."

"She said he told her who he was and that he was cutting her to show her mother what he would do if she married again."

"Well, that sounds like Jules Donagan all right. I try not to judge, but it was always true. If there was something he could do to hurt someone, he did it."

"We younger kids thought it was pretty cool, the way he wasn't afraid to get in trouble at school. I suppose that's why Kate married him when she came back from her nurse studies. He could be appealing when he wanted to."

Caroline cut a piece of tender beef carefully. "Maybe so. I never saw anything appealing about him. Even when he was a kid, I used to see him skulking in the woods back of the house. Let me tell you, I watched him closely, especially if you were playing in the yard."

"The man he killed before he ran away was not exactly a

town leader type, was he?"

"It was a man just like him by the general gossip. A stranger in Sawtown. A drifter. They fought over a poker game."

"Sounds like one of the old westerns we used to see."

"Except that now we call murder by its right name no matter who gets killed. But, yes, the commotion here in town was a lot like the westerns. The sheriff got up a posse and they combed these woods for months, but Jules had spent so much time in there he knew every place to hide, and they never found him. Now people think he left the country. I suppose he's still listed in police computers even though it's been eight years now since he ran away, and he's been legally declared dead."

"So that Kate can marry again?"

Caroline nodded. "That killing took away much of Kate's life, too. Not that it was so good with Jules Donagan, but if he had been the man he should have been, she wouldn't have had to drive to work in the hospital in Clifton every day to support Julie. Thank goodness, now that you're here, she can work at the clinic and spend more time with Julie. And with Al, once they're married."

"Al? I thought his name was. . ."

"Alden Ferris. My boss. He and his sister bought the Blue Bird Cafe when Con Conyer died. They're from Boston. They came through here on vacation a few years ago and fell in love with this country. Who did you think she was marrying?"

"The bum type who brought Julie in. She introduced him as Matthew Barnes."

"Matthew? Matthew Barnes brought her in? Bum type? Honey, he's the new owner of Morgan Lumber. And the furniture factory."

"Well, he acted awfully concerned about Julie, and he seemed to be close enough to them to decide on his own to take Julie to Clifton before telling Kate she'd been hurt."

"He probably thought he was being considerate of Kate. No matter how thoughtful they are, men who've never had children of their own can't understand how a mother feels." Emily was surprised at Caroline's vehemence.

"Then where does he fit into the situation?" Even as she asked, Emily assured herself that she was just making conversation.

"He and Alden are best friends. He did help Kate get Jules declared dead, and he and Julie have a very special feeling about each other, but he's never been anything but friends with Kate. Matthew goes into the woods and works with his men or plans the cuts sometimes. He doesn't dress like a businessman then."

So that was the man who directed the saws that cut all the trees from a whole hillside and let it slide down into the river, Emily thought. Maybe she had been right in her first reaction to him.

They were in the middle of a leisurely dessert of coffee and chocolate cream pie piled high with meringue when a car pulled into the yard.

"Probably just somebody lost," Caroline said. "Every once in awhile someone misses the dead end sign, where our lane joins the county road, and ends up in my yard. I don't mind except at 2 o'clock in the morning. Come to think of it, now that I'm in the back bedroom, you're going to get the headlight reflections on the ceiling now."

"It won't bother me. My sleep habits have turned into 'if you're off your feet and not driving, sleep while you can.' But, Mom, somebody's getting out, I think."

Caroline stood up and moved to the door. "Sometimes I have to tell them where—oh, it's Ben."

"Maybe it's something about Kate's husband."

"Maybe." Caroline smiled, almost secretively, Emily thought, as she opened the door.

Ben was a big man with a hearty voice. Though he was probably only in his fifties, his hair had been pure white as long as Emily could remember. He looked at Caroline now with a warm concern in his eyes.

It took Emily a few minutes to recognize the man with him as the bewhiskered woodsman who had stopped her on the road with a crying child in his arms. The clean lines of Matthew Barnes' face were clear of whiskers. He was dressed in a soft, open-throated shirt and slacks that accented the height and muscular strength that had caused her car to suddenly become smaller when he got in it. His dark eyes were more tranquil now, and a smile warmed his face as he met her eyes across the room.

"Caroline, we want you and the doc to come stay in town till we can sort out this business about Jules Donagan," Ben said, without preamble. "If he's somewhere back in the forest, you may be in danger."

Caroline didn't answer him directly. "Come in, Ben. You too, Matthew. I've got your favorite pie."

"Evenin', Doc." Ben walked through the little living room

to the table as though he were a familiar visitor here. He pulled up one leaf of the table and he and Matthew Barnes found chairs. Emily wasn't sure how it happened, but she found herself with the same feeling of suddenly shrunken space as Matthew settled a few inches from her. Caroline served them pie and coffee before she answered Ben's request.

"Now, Ben, Emily is just home today and we've looked forward to this far too long to uproot her already. And I've known that smart aleck kid too long to be afraid of him."

"If Jules Donagan is hiding out there somewhere, he's not the kid you knew. For your own protection, you must move into town." Matthew Barnes' deep voice held that same expectation of obedience that Emily had heard earlier in her car. And her reaction was the same.

"We're adults and quite capable of making our own decisions, Mr. Barnes." She deliberately answered in the clearly concise voice she used in giving orders for her patients.

Matthew Barnes liked meeting someone who challenged him even in his business, though he expected his final decisions to be followed. This woman who looked like the young shepherdess in a picture book his mother used to read to him, with her soft brown hair and wide chocolate eyes, enthralled him. He had no idea when he helped plan the clinic that the doctor they expected would be so lovely. But he had quickly accepted her as a good doctor when he had watched her stitch up young Julie with an economy of movement and seen the concern in her eyes.

He admired proficiency whether it was in cutting his walnut, oak, and pine to get the best of the grain, fashioning that wood into fine furniture, or suturing a child's wound so it would make a minimal scar. But he also recognized pure stubbornness when he saw it. He decided to concentrate on Caroline's delicious pie and let Ben talk for awhile.

"Now, Caroline, I know how you feel about this house. Goodness knows, you've told me plenty of times. But it wouldn't hurt you to leave it for a day or two while we check out this Jules Donagan thing."

Caroline snorted inelegantly. "A day or two. You know, Ben, he can hide out back in those hills and trees for a year or two."

"The county sheriff's bringing in a search group with dogs to help us," Matthew said, "and I have all my men looking for any sign of him while they work."

Emily's brown eyes suddenly flashed. "Just how long will it take them to cut enough trees down that nothing has a place to hide?" she asked in a deceptively mild voice.

Her question took the flavor out of the last bite of Matthew's pie. So she was one of those people who thought that touching a saw to a tree was a violation. He had a degree in forestry. He had studied modern methods of forest management and used them, but he made it a practice not to respond to such remarks and he certainly wasn't going to defend himself to this child who called herself a doctor.

But Ben did it for him. "Now, Emily," he said. "Morgan Lumber isn't what it used to be when your dad worked for the company."

"And died for it." Emily's voice was much too bitter to

be talking about something that happened so long ago.

Caroline brought the conversation back to the present. "We're staying here tonight for sure, Ben. We'll talk about it tomorrow."

Ben looked at her with mild exasperation. "I know that tone, Caroline. Well, I'll have Dave check on you, so don't be disturbed if you hear his car. Anyway, thanks for the pie and coffee. Delicious as usual. See you, Emily." He and Matthew stood up to go. "Oh, glad you're here, Doctor Emily Richards, and Sawtown is proud of you."

Emily and Caroline stood up, too. "Thanks, Ben, I'm glad to be here."

Emily felt a twinge of guilt. Was she being unfair not to tell everyone that she would be in Sawtown only long enough to fulfill her promise?

Lying in bed later, listening to the familiar noises outside, she assured herself that it was better not to talk about leaving yet. She'd already laid the groundwork with Joyce to take her place—if Joyce didn't change her mind under her father's pressure. If that happened, she'd just have to find someone else.

She wondered vaguely what Ryan and Joyce were doing back in the hospital just before she drifted off into a sound sleep.

four

Emily thought she might have heard Dave's car once in the night, but she didn't really wake completely. Nor could she remember dreaming. Her first night back at home was relaxed and restful, with no anxiety about the possibility of Jules Donagan's presence somewhere in the forest.

She woke to a profound silence in the house; Caroline had already left for work. Used to waking to sounds of the city outside her small apartment or of the hospital when she slept in one of the on call rooms, Emily found the silence strange but pleasantly familiar.

Out in the kitchen she found some coffee and started it bubbling up in her mother's old-fashioned percolator, while she poured milk on a bowl of cereal. Later, she decided, she would get out the new cappuccino machine she'd gifted herself with for finishing her residency.

She added juice and took it all out to the small deck on the back of the house, directly overlooking the forest, which started at the end of Caroline's newly plowed and carefully tended vegetable garden.

In spite of the fact that it had taken her father, Emily had learned a love of the forest from her mother. She remembered how Caroline had taught her to "listen to its silence" until she learned to appreciate that, from the tiny "chuck chucks" of ground squirrels to the yip of a fox, the noises of native life were a part of the forest and blended with rather than broke its silence. Even the possibility that Jules Donagan might be hiding somewhere in its depths on this sunny morning didn't change that.

She ate slowly, reveling in the movement and shadows in front of her. Birds darted in and out of the trees and onto the sloping back lawn. Blue jays argued with squirrels about ownership of the lawn and some leftovers that Caroline had put out before she went to work. As Emily watched, a small woodchuck ventured out to investigate the spoils.

The telephone interrupted her pleasant interlude. For a minute Emily considered not answering, but the thought that it might be Kate looking for her made her go in and pick up Caroline's kitchen phone.

"Emily," Ryan's familiar, hurried voice greeted her. "I only have a minute before I go on duty, but I needed to hear your voice and know that you got home all right. I wanted to call you last night, but you know what happens to a resident's plans."

"Guess what? That kind of thing happens when you get out of residency, too." Emily told him briefly of her experience with Kate and Julie. She surprised herself by not mentioning Matthew Barnes.

Ryan zeroed in on Jules Donagan. "Are you out there in that house that's practically in the forest? And a murderer is hiding out there somewhere? Emily, how quickly can you find a place in town?"

"That's what—" Emily hesitated, "—Ben, the police chief, asked. Mom and I don't want to leave, but she promised Ben that we'd talk about it when she gets off work today."

"When she gets off work. Emily, are you there alone now?"

"Well, except for some birds and squirrels and such."

"Listen, I've got to go and I want to hang up and let you get away from there anyway. He could be right outside. You could be in danger, Emily."

Emily laughed. "Listen, city boy, I don't think my birds and woodchucks would be going about their business so quietly if someone was skulking in the edge of the forest. I don't feel in danger, Ryan. But I want to go into the clinic anyway. I can't wait to check it out."

"Don't learn to like it too much. You know where we want you to be when you're Mrs. Ryan Page."

Emily quickly ended the conversation. She didn't need to explain to Ryan again that she wouldn't talk about marriage until she was free to join him in Africa.

She dressed in a white blouse and cheery printed skirt, slipped flats on bare feet, and ran a comb through her short hair. As she went out to her car, she felt a childish desire to skip in response to the morning. How could there be danger in such a perfect world?

There were few people on the street in Sawtown, but that wasn't unusual. Most of the residents would be at work, either at the mill or in the new factory in back of the clinic, which her mother had said employed women and older lumberjacks as well as some young people.

There were only a few cars in the parking lot of the Blue Bird Cafe, but Emily was sure that at least one table was filled with retired lumber workers who met to tell tall tales and reminisce. Later, on a day like this they would move to a bench in the tiny park further down the street to whittle and continue their lazy conversations.

Emily turned down the side street and parked her car at the clinic. She took a moment to admire the solid-looking red brick building before she looked at the only other car in the lot, wondering if it belonged to Kate. She wasn't sure Kate would be here after yesterday's unsettling incident.

The door was locked and since she still didn't have a key, Emily pressed the button beside a small sign which said RING FOR EMERGENCIES.

In a few minutes she heard a sound inside, and Kate opened the door. Emily stepped into the waiting room. Apparently Kate had been here quite awhile for chairs and tables had been delivered and placed about the walls of the rectangular room. A small TV sat high on a shelf near the door leading to the exam and treatment rooms.

"It's beginning to look like a real clinic," Emily said, admiring the pleasantly bright blues and whites of the walls and furnishings. "Did you choose the colors?"

"With a little help from everyone in town," Kate said, laughing. "The people of Sawtown treat the clinic like a favorite child. It's their baby and they all feel like they own it. And you, I'm afraid."

Again Emily fought off a sense of guilt. But surely she wouldn't have such a strong desire to go to the mission field if that wasn't what God wanted for her. And He would help her find a doctor for this town and this clinic. She moved to examine the receptionist desk that sat behind a low curved counter, shaking off her unpleasant thoughts.

"I'm anxious to get to work. When will it be ready to open?" Emily sat down on a comfortable office chair behind the desk and looked across the counter at the waiting room as though she were seeing patients waiting there for her healing touch.

"On Monday, if you're ready. That will give you today and tomorrow and Sunday to settle in." Kate sat on a corner of the counter, swinging one slim blue jeaned leg. "Well, actually Sunday, after church, Sawtown is going to hold an open house for you with dinner in the parking lot. At first we were going to surprise you, but Ben and Matthew and I convinced them that you might want to know ahead of time. After all, we didn't want to have a party for someone who might be out somewhere else." Kate hesitated. "I hope you don't mind. They really want to show you how proud they are of you and how glad they are to have you here."

"I'm touched," Emily said, honestly. Then she laughed. "I see Sawtown hasn't changed its habit of feeding itself a big dinner at every opportunity."

"No, they haven't," Kate agreed, smiling. "Maybe that's why the Blue Bird has done so well all these years."

Emily looked at Kate with concern. "Mom told me that you're planning to marry the new owner. I guess I shouldn't say congratulations just yet. How is Julie this morning?"

"Nervous. She cried a lot last night. I planned to bring her in with me today, but she was still asleep when I left and Bessie promised not to take her eyes off her. We live in an upstairs apartment in Bessie Moore's house. Bessie lives downstairs. You remember her?"

Emily nodded.

"She's in her seventies now, but she's crazy about Julie and still thinks she's a match for anyone who wants to hurt her. Maxine, Al's sister, said she'd go out later this morning. She spends a lot of time with Julie."

"You look like you may not be too happy about that."

"Did I? I didn't mean to. It's just that. . .Maxine is a lot older than Alden. She raised him, actually, after their parents died. Alden, of course, feels a lot of appreciation for her and I try to, also, but I do wish she wasn't so attached to him. Though I suppose I should be glad she's kept him from marrying." Kate laughed nervously. "He says he didn't know anyone until me who was worth fighting for. Now, I don't know. . ." She let the sentence trail off, looking at the blue-and-white squares of the floor.

Emily let the silence lie for awhile, then asked, "Do you want to talk about Jules?"

Kate grimaced. "I wish I didn't have to think about him. You know I can't pray that he's dead, but I didn't sleep at all last night. There just doesn't seem to be an answer. I love Alden so much and we were so happy. I'm scared."

A quick memory of sitting beside Peggy Green in the hospital in St. Louis flicked through Emily's mind. So many times compassionate listening was the only thing she could offer.

Kate brought herself back to the present. "Well, I'm just waiting for whatever God and Ben work out. I'm not bragging that I've succeeded, but I'm trying to wait quietly. And it helps to have this work to do. Want to see the rest of the clinic?"

Emily stood, then sat down again abruptly as she glanced at a table beside her. "We have a computer system? I had no idea we would be able to afford anything like that. I've been prepared to work with bare bones."

"We have an angel," Kate laughed. "An anonymous

angel."

The name of Matthew Barnes ran through Emily's mind, but Kate insisted that there was a real mystery about the identity of the donor.

A tour of the clinic showed that the donor had given them a great deal more than a computer. There was an observation room equipped with a hospital bed as well as an electrocardiogram machine, a heart monitor, and a respirator. Emily could keep a heart attack victim safe in this room until an ambulance could come from Clifton. She could even keep someone here and watch them overnight if she needed to. Thinking of all the lives this equipment could save in the coming years, Emily could only breathe a "thank You" to God and whoever donated it.

More surprises were to come. After going through two examination rooms, Kate led her into a room where gleaming X-ray equipment waited. Emily recognized a mammogram machine and smiled in delight. She or Kate could take simple pictures, but Emily immediately made mental plans to get a technician to come in to take mammograms and make arrangements with a radiologist to read them. Emily was sure that few women in Sawtown actually made the trip to Clifton for such things as mammograms.

"Kate, this is great," she said. "Are you going to show me a lab, too?"

"How did you guess? This way, please."

The lab was across the hall and contained the basic equipment for simple tests. "Just what we need," Emily said after inspecting it.

Farther back was a small office for Kate and a larger

one for her. At the very end of the building was a galley type kitchen with a microwave, refrigerator, coffee pot, and hot plate on a counter beside a small table and chairs. There was a narrow exit door at the side that Emily and Kate could use as a private entrance.

"That angel expects us to spend long hours at the clinic," Kate observed.

"How can that angel pretend anonymity when there's only one possible person who can afford these things?"

"You're thinking Matthew Barnes, aren't you? Well, some of the extras may have come from him, but not all. He's apparently not a zillionaire and the mill and factory have a lot of money tied up. Anyway, the town built and bought the basic equipment for the clinic by floating a bond. So it really is a community project."

"But where did Matthew Barnes come from? He wasn't here when I lived here and—"

Before she could finish her question, a male voice from the front called out, "Kate?"

Kate went to the front and Emily followed. Matthew Barnes stood just inside the door to the waiting room that Kate had left unlocked when she let Emily in.

"Kate, I just came by to see how you're doing," he began, then saw Emily and smiled. "Morning, Doc. Inspecting your kingdom?"

Emily found herself responding to that smile with a little catch in her throat that made it hard to answer. It was a smile that seemed to invite her in, give her a comfortable chair, and offer her a cup of tea.

"And quite a kingdom it is," she managed to say. "Much, much more than I expected to have to start with."

"Good. That way you know how much Sawtown appreciates you." If he had furnished the extras himself, he was being awfully good at hiding it.

Emily, hoping she was successfully hiding a bit of curiosity about Matthew's unusual concern for Kate, who was engaged to another man, excused herself and left.

Matthew watched her walk across to her car. He was uncomfortably aware that she probably did think he had bought the extras for the clinic, but he hadn't. Matthew had worked for other people after he graduated from forestry school. His own savings plus a small inheritance and a surprisingly large insurance policy when his father followed his mother in death had given him the money to buy the economically troubled Morgan Lumber. He had started Sawtown Furniture on a loan when he realized how much the town needed another industry. Though he supported the clinic and had worked for it, he didn't have the free money to buy the extras. And he didn't know who did, any more than the other town residents.

Watching Emily wheel her car out to the street, he found himself wanting to be totally open with her. He must find some way to make her know that, much as he wished he could be, he wasn't the unknown donor.

Once away from the clinic, Emily decided to go into the Blue Bird Cafe for a cup of coffee since she was so close. She admitted to a large lump of curiosity about Alden Ferris, Kate's intended husband, as well as a friendly urge to see the place where her mother had worked for so many years.

It was little different from a million other small town cafes. An oval counter with high, plastic-covered stools ran across the front. Tables were scattered in the center and black plastic booths lined the wall.

Emily took a stool at the counter and was face to face with a refrigerated case of her mother's gorgeous cream and delicately browned fruit pies. Groaning, she gave in and ordered a piece of apple.

She didn't see either her mother or anyone who might be Alden Ferris. She didn't know the woman behind the counter. She was a large woman, probably in her early fifties, dressed in an unfitted dark dress that looked too hot for the season. Her face was impassive, neither friendly nor unfriendly, as she got coffee and the pie of Emily's choice with an economy of sure movements that Emily admired.

"Is Caroline busy?" Emily asked, feeling a strange sense of insecurity for someone who had run in and out of the Blue Bird kitchen since she was a child.

"Probably not too busy to talk." The woman had a deep voice and clipped accent that was foreign to Sawtown. Emily guessed that she must be Maxine Ferris. The woman stepped to the service window and called, "Caroline."

Immediately, Caroline's smiling face appeared at the window. She waved gaily to Emily. "I was just thinking of a cup of coffee. I'll be right out."

In a moment, Caroline came out and poured herself a cup of coffee. She took her place beside Emily, while waving and saying "Hello" to the scattered patrons.

She exchanged good-natured comments with the table of men who, usually engaged in measuring the length of fish lost off long gone hooks or the size of long felled trees, were now talking in unrestrained tones about Jules

Donagan.

They broke off to speak to Caroline, and their easygoing comments showed respect and friendliness for her. Emily remembered that a few of the single ones had tried to date Caroline but she, so far as Emily knew, had never been interested in anyone since her husband's death.

"Maxine, this is my daughter, Dr. Emily Richards." Caroline's voice held a great deal of pride. "Emily, Maxine Ferris."

Emily exchanged greetings with Maxine Ferris, mentally congratulating herself that she had guessed right about her identity.

"Welcome home, Dr. Richards," called one of the men at the old lumberjack's table. "We've waited a good long time for you."

There were murmurs of agreement from other tables. Emily gave them all a cheery wave and nod of thanks, then turned her attention to her mother's pie, which was as delicious as always. She promised herself that now that she wasn't going to be running through long miles of hospital corridors anymore, she would curtail her appreciation of Caroline's pies in the interest of keeping her figure.

The thought reminded her that she should take a day as soon as possible to go into Clifton and finish the procedure of admission to the hospital staff there, which she had started while still in St. Louis. She would also need to become acquainted with specialty physicians there to call on when she had a patient that needed surgery or other special treatment or diagnosis. She knew Dr. Anderson, who had performed most of Sawtown's surgery for years, and knew she could refer patients to him. She was sure he would help her select other good specialists.

After talking with Caroline for a bit and eliciting a few abrupt comments from Maxine Ferris, Emily finished her coffee.

"I'm cooking tonight," she told her mother. "Probably on the grill."

"Good. It's already out on the patio and cleaned for the summer."

Emily nodded, but she was somewhat surprised. Usually her mother, who didn't use the portable grill herself, left it in the storeroom except when Emily was home for a visit. She gave the usual pleasantries to Maxine, who responded with a jerk of the head as she went to take an order from another customer.

Maxine Ferris certainly is an unusual character to find in Sawtown, Emily reflected as she drove home. She suspected that it was her brother's idea to move to Sawtown and Maxine only came because she wanted to be near him. She found herself feeling a little sorry for Kate, who was getting her for a sister-in-law, and hoped that Alden wasn't like her. Kate certainly deserved better for a husband.

Reminded of Kate's almost unbearable situation with Jules, she said a short prayer that whatever happened, it would be good for Kate and Julie. As she pulled into her driveway, her thoughts wandered to Ryan and then, to her surprise and slight resentment, to Matthew Barnes. Determinedly, she pulled them back to Ryan. He would probably call tonight. With a wistful melancholy, she remembered that he would be leaving soon for Africa. In spite of her pleasant welcome to Sawtown, she longed to go with him.

five

"There's a church in the valley by the wildwood. . . ." Emily let the words of the song run through her mind as Caroline parked her car in the cramped clearing by their church. The song could have been written about this little church with its old-fashioned bell tower and white clapboard siding that needed frequent volunteer painting work.

It snuggled between two gentle hills just outside town, and when the church members weren't busy painting it, they were busy keeping the forest from retaking its lawn and cemetery. In fact, the Reverend Ethan Adams' call to volunteerism was second only to his call to godliness.

This Sunday was no exception. "We've set this coming Saturday to clean our cemetery for Memorial Day."

Reverend Adams stood at the small but beautifully carved and polished pulpit. His thin, wiry body and white hair seemed exactly like they did when Emily left. "Bring your own rakes and machetes. Quite a few vines have sprung up since last fall."

He hesitated and cleared his throat, then continued, his soft voice seeming to deepen as it always did when he wanted the full attention of his audience. "Now we have a problem that's sprung up in our community, too, like poison vines. One of our wayward sons that we have thought was in the hands of God now seems to be causing trouble

as he did years ago. I want to remind you that his wife and
child need our Christian support and not our gossip. So
let's keep them in our prayers and off our tongues this
week. And unless Ben or the sheriff puts you in his posse,
don't go into the forest looking for him.

"Now don't forget the dinner to welcome our old friend
and new doctor, our own grown-up Miss Emily. We'll meet
on the grounds of the clinic right after church, giving ourselves time to go home or to the Blue Bird and get that
good food we know is stashed away and that we're all
looking forward to."

Emily almost lost herself in memories of growing up
listening to Reverend Adams' easy country talk, so different from the big church she had attended, when possible,
in St. Louis. She was brought back by the call to stand and
the enthusiastic swing of the parishioners into the simple
cadence of "Love Lifted Me."

She was nostalgically warmed to see Angeline, the Reverend Adams' happily plump wife, looking benevolently
over the congregation while playing the organ for the hymns
from memory.

As she joined the singing, she noticed Kate standing a
few rows in front of her. Next to her was a tall man Emily
didn't know, but she did recognize the broad, ungraceful
lines of Maxine Ferris beside him. Julie slumped on Kate's
other side. Perhaps purposely, Dave Willis and Matthew
Barnes sat at each end, forming a barrier against anyone
else sitting in that pew. Strangely, Emily thought, Ben had
sat down next to Caroline when he came in, instead of near
Julie.

Emily found herself studying Julie's body language,

which seemed to scream out unhappiness and despair. She must talk to Kate about getting Julie in to someone in Clifton for counseling or, failing that, try to help her herself.

She scolded herself for letting her mind wander as they waited quietly for the sermon. Reverend Adams read to them from Psalm 56:

> "'When I am afraid
> I will put my trust in Thee.
> In God, whose word I praise,
> In God I have put my trust:
> I shall not be afraid.
> What can mere man do to me?'"

Then he read Jesus' words to them, "'For I was hungry and you gave me something to eat; I was thirsty and you gave me drink; I was a stranger and you invited me in; naked, and you clothed me; I was sick and you visited me: I was in prison, and you came to me.'"

Reverend Adams spoke plainly to them as only a leader who had lived among his people for many years could, naming Kate and Julie openly and reminding them again that they must support them.

Emily left the church feeling almost as if she had never been away from Sawtown. The openness between Reverend Adams and the church members made her think of those almost unused words, "the flock," and took her back to her childhood when she had listened to him gently chastise or enthusiastically praise church members for their actions.

Caroline, as well as many others of the church members, had left food keeping hot or cold in the ovens and refrigerators of the Blue Bird Cafe. As the man who had been sitting with Kate in church opened the cafe doors and greeted them, Emily knew that her earlier guess that this was Alden Ferris was correct. Caroline introduced them.

"Dr. Richards, I've heard a bit about you." In spite of his clipped accent, his voice was warm and his wide grin was friendly.

Emily returned his firm handshake. "I've heard your name mentioned, too," she said, smiling.

Alden Ferris was tall and extremely thin. He stood with a slight bend to his shoulders, as if he had been giving in to gravity or the pull of someone else all his life. Emily guessed, looking at his stolid sister, that she was the pressure he leaned against. She felt an instant liking for him— a liking, she admitted to herself, she found hard to feel for his sister.

She helped Caroline carry containers of food out to the car and drove the short distance to the clinic so Caroline could hold an especially fragile pie carefully in her hands.

The back of the parking area of the clinic was filled with long boards placed on trestles and covered with white paper, shiny in the strong sunlight. They were soon covered with dishes piled high with chicken, beef, and a seemingly unending variety of vegetables, salads, and desserts, as people from all the churches in town arrived, lining the street and the parking lot of Sawtown Furniture with cars and looking for places to put yet more food.

After grace was said, the food seemed to disappear as quickly as it had appeared, with much friendly talk and laughter. Some of the younger ones sat on car hoods; some spilled over onto the grounds of the furniture factory. Children found more appeal in racing about the edges of the crowd in some kind of game that only they recognized than in eating or settling down for the dedication service.

Julie didn't join them but stayed close to Kate. Young Dave Willis stayed close to both of them in what, Emily guessed, he thought was a discrete, professional tail, but wasn't. Bessie Moore, Kate's landlord and baby-sitter, had arrived from her own church and stuck just as closely, while giving Dave unfriendly looks that said as plainly as words that he was not only not needed but was trespassing on her territory.

Emily and Caroline moved through the crowd. Emily greeted old friends and was introduced to a few new faces. The hospital at St. Louis seemed very far away. But not Ryan, not the wish to go to the mission field, she reminded herself, as she unwillingly met Matthew's smiling gaze and found herself smiling back.

After the food, the crowd stayed by the tables or rested on the grass to hear a talented youthful trio sing folk and traditional religious songs to the accompaniment of a guitar. Then there was a short dedication speech by Mayor Art Armstrong, who was an expert sawyer for Morgan Lumber when not performing his scant duties as mayor. After a dedicatory prayer from Reverend Adams, Emily stayed by the door of the waiting room to greet people while Kate, Alden, and Matthew shared the task of taking groups through to show off the clinic.

The obvious strain between Bessie Moore and Maxine Ferris, who now flanked Julie on a waiting room couch while Dave pretended to be casually looking out the window near them, made Emily somewhat uncomfortable. Still, she was relieved to know that Julie was being protected, though Maxine, a strangely satisfied expression on her face, seemed to be more occupied in watching people wander in and out of the back rooms.

The thought ran through Emily's mind that she had not yet seen Julie smile. Then another thought wormed its way behind her own beginning-to-crack smile. Among the last of the crowd to enter was Caroline and Ben. Together. Somehow, they seemed to be together a lot.

In spite of the Reverend Adams' warning sermon, many of those who came in and went out past Emily were talking in low tones about Jules Donagan lurking in the forest.

"I don't care what the Reverend says," one middle-aged lady said to another as they stepped out after pretending not to stare at the three on the couch. "We have to talk about what we're to do if we're all murdered in our beds."

Emily felt her smile becoming real as they moved away before she could hear the other lady's solution. Then it died away as she saw Kate's face, strained with fatigue and the effort of trying to appear natural with the curious and frightened townspeople.

"Kate, are you sure you want to try to come in tomorrow?" Emily asked in a low voice after everyone except Alden, Matthew Barnes, and Julie and her guard had left. "I can stumble around and find things myself. We shouldn't have many patients the first day anyway."

Kate managed a tired smile. "Dr. Richards, ma'am, half the town will be in here tomorrow. Everybody who can scrape up an ache or pain will drop in to see how the new doc works. I'll be here. Julie is being watched," she added in a low tone.

"But," Emily glanced at Julie's withdrawn face, "maybe she needs you, Kate."

"Al and I will spend this evening with her. We'll just eat a pizza at home and watch a movie together. She used to like that."

"Used to?"

Kate looked concerned. "She was so happy about getting a new father for awhile. Then, about a month ago, she changed toward Al. That's why we've been holding off our marriage, hoping she'll change back. Now, I guess it's lucky we did. I'd hate to be a bigamist." Kate's eyes told Emily she was wholly serious.

"Kate, don't." Al Ferris's face showed his concern. "You know that Ben and Sheriff Carnes doubt that Jules is actually back. Even if he's alive, why should he suddenly care what you do after all this time?"

"Then, who?" Kate sounded desperate, as if she had come to the end of her taut nerves.

"I don't know," Al said. "But I know that I'll fight whoever it is for you, Kate. Whoever it is." Emily thought he stood a little more erect than usual. "Let's take Julie home. I'll get a pizza from the cafe and we can cook it in your oven. Bessie can ride with us. Maxine has her own car here."

Kate, looking relieved to have someone take over, went to gather the group together. As they went out, Emily noticed that Caroline didn't seem to be there anymore. In fact no one was there except Matthew Barnes.

"I promised Kate we'd lock up and I'd give you this key," he said. "Also, your mom said come home for leftovers."

Emily looked surprised. "But Mom and I came in the same car. I don't have mine."

"No problem." Matthew grinned. "She invited me to come out for leftovers, too. We can go together." Emily had noticed before that he had an instant make-you-like-him grin. But what was her mother thinking of to practically shove them together?

Reluctantly, she returned his smile. "I guess I have no choice," she said. "But I'm surprised that Mom left without telling me."

"You've been pretty well surrounded with well-wishers who are touchingly relieved to have a doctor here. The people of this community have had to drive to Clifton or further for medical care for much too long." He spoke seriously and the thought ran quickly through her mind that one Dr. Ryan Page was leaving tomorrow for Africa and the countdown till she could join him would begin. *But I will find another doctor*, she reminded herself.

"What do we have to do to lock up?" she asked.

"Just close this door behind us. I've already turned out the lights in back."

The sunlight was slanting on the only car in sight, so it didn't require Matthew's walking toward it to conclude that it was his. What was hard was believing that the rather battered looking Chevy was the car a man like Matthew would drive.

He caught her look of surprise. "Well, I do have a second car," he said, opening the passenger door with a flourish, "but it's not as fancy or new as this one. Matter of fact it's a ten-year-old Jeep. I drive it back in the forest."

Emily pulled the seat belt forward and fastened it as he

moved around to the driver's seat and started the car. She wished he hadn't mentioned the lumber business just when she was starting to feel comfortable with him.

But he had something else on his mind now. "Have you and Caroline talked about moving into town till Ben can get the answer to this Jules Donagan thing?" he asked as he turned onto the county road that was Main Street and headed out of town.

"Not really. We've sort of ignoring the subject. Neither of us wants to leave home."

"Well, we're going to discuss it tonight," he said a bit grimly.

"Why? It's really. . ." she wanted to add something about it being none of his business, but changed it to a more diplomatic, "our decision."

"Let's just say I don't want Sawtown's new doctor to be hurt. You're needed."

"Well, can you think of any reason Jules Donagan, if he is still alive, would want to hurt me? Anyway, Alden said that Ben doesn't really believe that he is around."

"It doesn't seem likely. But we have to act like he is till we know if it is him, or if it isn't, who would want to hurt Julie. Or who would want to keep Kate and Al from getting married."

You? Emily wondered. *You seem to be awfully close to Kate. Are you the point of a triangle that got lopped off?* Looking at the smooth, strong line of his jaw now, she remembered her suspicions the first time she saw him. Then she told herself such suspicions were ridiculous. Matthew Barnes might not be her favorite person, but he surely wasn't a child slasher.

She remembered the overheard question of "what are we to do if we get murdered in our beds" and repeated it to Matthew. They were still laughing about it when he pulled into her driveway.

"Isn't that Ben's car?" she asked, in concern. "Why do you suppose he's here? Is something wrong?"

"Obviously," Matthew said dryly, as he turned off the ignition, "you and Caroline need to talk about more than whether or not to move into town."

Ben and Caroline were seated in lawn chairs on the patio, each with a soft drink can in their hand. They seemed to be sitting in a comfortable silence, watching the birds among the trees.

Caroline turned and smiled when Matthew and Emily walked out, but didn't get up. "Well, come along and join us. We're just letting ourselves relax from all the people. You probably need it more than we do. Emily, there's tea or soft drinks in the refrigerator."

"I think I feel like coffee, Mom. I'll make it." Emily suddenly didn't want to be a part of that comfortable ambiance on the patio. Matthew opted for coffee, too, and Emily insisted that he sit down and wait while she fixed it. She wanted to be alone for awhile and decided to take the extra time to make cappuccino. She had already unpacked her machine.

What was the feeling between Ben and her mom? And why hadn't she been told if it was something more than friendship? Emily wasn't sure of her own feelings. She had just taken it for granted for so long that Caroline chose to live alone. Now something that had been a certainty was seeming to change.

And was that why Caroline had so openly thrown her and Matthew together today? So she could be with Ben? Yet Caroline knew about Ryan, if not about all their plans.

When the coffee and milk were ready, she filled two mugs with the frothy ambrosia and slivered chocolate on top. She carried the mugs out and sat down on the only empty chair, beside Matthew. She was instantly aware that the comfortable atmosphere had changed.

"But, Caroline, Bessie can let you rent a couple of rooms till we know for sure about Jules Donagan."

"Julie was playing in Bessie's yard when she was taken and hurt," Caroline pointed out. "Why would we be any better off there?"

"Because I've got that house being watched every minute," Ben replied. "Sheriff Carnes has let me borrow enough deputies to take over, when Dave will let them."

Caroline stood up abruptly. "You'll have to show me Jules Donagan walking out of those trees with a knife in his hand before I see any reason to move into town," she said earnestly. "Now, sandwiches are about to be made in the kitchen. I'll bring them out."

The three of them were left in a sort of uncertain silence. Then Ben sighed. "I suppose you agree with her, Doc?"

"Absolutely," Emily answered. "Mom and I have lived out here too long to be afraid of anything in the forest."

"I would have thought that the years in St. Louis might make you more aware of the danger people are to each other," Matthew said.

Emily smiled. "It did. But it also made me realize that this is the way the world is today and if we let ourselves live in constant fear, we stop living."

Ben grunted. "I guess I can't argue with that, Doc Emily. But I'll still send someone out to check on you frequently."

"By the way," Matthew changed the subject, "cappuccino coffee with chocolate happens to be one of my favorite beverages and I haven't had any for much too long. Thanks."

Emily let a smile answer him and leaned back in her chair, enjoying her own drink.

Ben and Matthew talked a bit about the situation with Kate Donagan then until Caroline brought out a tray of sandwiches and pie. The atmosphere between the three slowly turned back to the easy give and take of old friends.

Emily listened without really hearing them. Careful not to let her gaze turn to Matthew's profile, she wondered if, under the easy conversation, he was aware of the strong current of strain between them.

Matthew took advantage of Emily's withdrawal to enjoy looking at her. If there was a strain between them, it was something he was determined to explore and eliminate. In his busy life, he had found little time for women and only in a few instances had he felt the attraction that he had for this small doctor.

Knowing that she was to be in Sawtown where he could take time to court her in an old-fashioned way was a delight to him, and he realized that was exactly what he planned to do.

Watching her, he noticed that there were tired lines in her face that made her look almost as old as he knew she really had to be. He set his mug and empty pie plate on the tray and stood up.

"Caroline, it was delicious. Doc Richards looks like she's

about to go to sleep and before she lets us feel like we're boring her, I'll help you clean up and leave."

Caroline laughed. "Never mind the cleaning, Matthew. It won't take a minute to wash these few dishes. Thanks for coming out and delivering Emily."

Matthew looked directly at Emily, who pulled herself upright in her chair and looked firmly into his eyes. "It was a pleasure," he said quietly.

He didn't wait for Emily to respond, but with a jaunty wave, walked around the side yard to his car. Emily wondered, in confusion, what she might have said if he had waited.

She was going to have to let him know about Ryan.

As though her thoughts had conjured him up, she heard the phone ring and knew, even before she answered, that it would be Ryan.

Caroline diplomatically put the dishes to drain and went to her room.

Though they talked for a long time and he put off saying good-bye, Emily felt like the miles between Arkansas and Africa already separated them.

After she hung up the phone she went back out and sat for a long time on the patio before going in to her room.

six

Kate was already in the clinic when Emily arrived at 8:00 on Monday. They had planned to start seeing patients at 9:00, but the early arrival of several women with children kept them from having time for any conversation.

Emily saw a few women with minimal complaints who obviously just wanted to be the first to be seen, and Emily was sure her exam tableside manner would be the subject of a few neighborly get-togethers in the next few days.

But she saw one child with a sore throat and ear infection that should have been taken care of at least a week before. The mother explained without seeming to feel sorry or apologetic that she just hadn't had time to take the child into Clifton. Emily remembered with a jolt that that was the general attitude when she was growing up in Sawtown. Even her own mother had sometimes failed to take her in to Clifton until a sore throat had become really bad.

While Kate gave the unhappy child a shot and she wrote a prescription for follow-up oral antibiotic, Emily determined to start praying now that Joyce or another doctor would be available to take her place in Sawtown.

Somehow there must be a way for the people of Sawtown to be taken care of while she went to the mission field where often there was no doctor in a nearby town and no money to pay if one were available.

They worked straight through the morning and ate sandwiches brought over by Alden at lunch time.

"I'm locking the door as I go out," Alden called. "Otherwise, neither one of you will take time to finish your lunch. Anybody really needing you will ring."

"I'll sneak out and open it again after he's gone," Kate whispered.

"Good," Emily said. "We can get everybody in the habit of giving us a lunch time later. I don't want them to think we're hard to contact now."

They sat on stools in the minuscule kitchen, drinking coffee. Kate opened one of the thick sandwiches Alden had brought and made a wry face.

"I told him tuna salad. He brings us enough beef to feed a bunch of sawyers. Sometimes I wonder if Al worries as much about my figure as he should."

Emily threw a critical look at Kate's super thin body. "Maybe he's noticed that you seem to have lost several pounds in the last few days. Kate, I haven't had time to say anything this morning, but I do want you to understand that I have some glimmering of the stress you're dealing with and I appreciate the fact that you come to work anyway."

"Thanks, Emily. I admit that sometimes the whole thing slams into my mind when I'm trying to take a patient history and I have to ask the same question twice. But I think I'd go crazy if I didn't have work to try to concentrate on."

"How does Julie feel about you coming to work? Is it bothering her?"

"No. If it was, if she clung to me or seemed to be afraid,

I'd stay with her. But she seems to be content staying with Bessie or having Maxine come by and pick her up and take her somewhere. And so far as I can tell she accepts that having someone from the sheriff's department around is enough. She doesn't seem to be scared at all." Kate sighed. "I almost wish she were. No, I don't want her to be scared, but to be. . .something. To show some emotion. . . be the little girl she was before. You haven't seen the real Julie, Emily."

Emily noticed that Kate seemed to have decided to call her Dr. Richards when a patient was around and Emily when they were alone. It seemed like a good routine.

She wondered if Kate might be ready to consider counseling for Julie. But before she could bring the subject up, they heard a call from the waiting room.

"Hello. Anybody here?"

Kate took a quick swallow of coffee. "Finish your lunch," she said. "I won't call you unless she's bleeding or blue." She hurried out and Emily heard her calm voice soothing an impatient woman at the front.

She ate her own sandwich and wrapped Kate's and placed it in the tiny refrigerator. Maybe later she could send Kate back to finish it.

It was still there Tuesday morning when Emily came in. She went to find Kate, who was seated at the front desk with an anxious frown on her face as she concentrated on unfinished insurance papers and charts that she had hurriedly stacked during yesterday's rush.

Emily pushed some papers back to make a place where she could safely lean against the desk. "Something has to change. You can't be the front desk person and the nurse both. Do you have any suggestions for a receptionist?"

"I do, Doctor. Cammie Johnson drives to Clifton every day to work in a doctor's office. We used to drive together. And it's true we need someone to be out front when I'm back helping you. If you want, I'll have her come in and talk to you this week."

"Good idea. Oh, and don't forget, today's the day to take Julie's stitches out."

"Maxine's already volunteered to bring her in this afternoon. I thought we might not be so busy then." She pushed some papers toward Emily. "Will you just sign these and I can take them back to my desk and deal with them later?"

Emily reached for a pen. "Maxine's being more helpful than I would have judged her to be. But then, I shouldn't let myself judge, should I? It just shows you what good advice the Bible gives us."

Kate laughed. Then she sobered. "Maxine gave her whole life to Al and I have to appreciate that, but she has dominated him and she's having a problem liking me. But she's crazy about Julie. I just hope she isn't going to try to make Julie take Al's place, since she very openly feels like she's losing him."

"What are your plans for living arrangements after you're married?"

Kate grimaced. "If we're married. Al's buying that new house you may have seen just out of town. Maxine will stay in the house by the Blue Bird where they live now. It was a part of the deal when they bought the cafe. Al hasn't said much about it, but I suspect they've had a few conversations about our plans."

"Do you think it's good for Maxine to spend so much time with Julie?"

"No, not really. But I have to think of Maxine, too. She's a lonely woman now. I don't want to take Julie away from her, too. And I know she won't intentionally do anything to hurt Julie."

A patient at the desk stopped the conversation, and they were as busy as the day before. The triviality of most of the complaints caused Emily some chagrin after being used to the life and death situations of a big teaching hospital, but she allowed them the option of checking out their new doctor. Many times, just being able to tell a doctor how they felt was healing. She said a brief prayer that she would always remember to listen, to really hear, what her patients had to say.

Then she let herself think for a minute of the desperate need she'd find in the mission field after her time here was up.

"We're getting everybody in Sawtown," Kate whispered laughingly to her as they passed between exam rooms. Then she sobered. "But I haven't see any of the country people yet."

While they were seeing the last patient of the day, Maxine Ferris brought Julie in. She came back with them to the exam room and though Emily would have ordinarily asked her to stay in the waiting room, she decided not to, since Kate didn't object to her being there.

"Well, Julie, let's see if you're going to have an interesting scar," Emily said as Maxine lifted Julie to the exam table.

Julie didn't answer. She sat with her head down as Kate unbuttoned her shirt and slipped it off. The dressings and wound were clean as Emily knew Kate would keep them. She quickly snipped the stitches and drew them out, watching Julie's expression more than the work she was doing with her hands. It didn't change from the solemn mask even when Emily knew she must have felt a twinge as the stitches came out.

She had cried that first day and clung to Kate, Emily remembered. Julie was rapidly withdrawing. All Kate's fears were real. She needed to get her into counseling.

"Okay, Puddin' Puss, that's it. I pronounce you cured," Kate said.

Julie raised her head at Kate's use of what was obviously a joking nickname that spoke of the closeness they had once shared. For a minute, Emily saw a different Julie. The mask was replaced by a joyous smile as she looked at her mother.

Then it faded as Maxine stepped forward and lifted her down. "We'll go over to the cafe and I'll fix us the biggest banana split in the world," she said.

Julie went with her quietly, but with none of the spontaneous joy Emily had seen in that one moment.

"I'll let you out the back door," Kate said. She gave Julie a quick hug as they went out and Emily thought she saw the thin body relax against her for just a moment before she pulled away.

Before Kate came back, Emily heard a masculine voice call out from the front. "Hello. Anybody home?"

She went out. When she saw who it was, she stopped behind the reception desk as though to put up a barrier.

Matthew Barnes had been listening carefully to the citizens of Sawtown about their new doctor, and he felt a surprising pleasure at the good things he heard. He had made a less-than-half-serious pretense that it was his bond to Sawtown that caused his interest. Watching her walk out to him now, he easily acknowledged that it was much more personal. He felt an intense desire to hold this doctor in his arms and make her realize that she was also a woman. He tried to block his thoughts from showing in his eyes.

"I've been hearing that you and Kate aren't eating right and I came to take you over to the Blue Bird and feed you, since we can't have our medical staff drooping from malnutrition." He wished she'd come out from behind that counter-desk.

"Nonsense. My mom feeds me bushels every night." Emily felt like she didn't dare move from her protective barrier, even if she kept Ryan's face in her mind like a shield.

She was rescued by Kate's arrival and Matthew repeated his invitation.

Kate looked at the desk where papers were stacked in several neat piles. "I need to work on these," she said. "Papers in a doctor's office have babies when we leave them alone at night."

Emily now found herself on Matthew's side. She knew how desperately Kate needed to get away and spend some time with Alden as much as to eat a good meal.

"Leave it now," she said. "After we eat, you can tell me

what to do and I'll help you."

"Just sign everything in triplicate, Dr. Richards," Kate answered, sighing. "Let's just leave our cars here and walk," she added, giving in.

Emily took time to call Caroline to tell her that she wouldn't be eating at home. She frowned slightly at Caroline's open pleasure to hear that she was eating with Matthew.

Maxine and Julie were already gone from the Blue Bird. "They took their banana splits home and took one for Bessie," Alden said, joining them at a back table. "And Dave followed them," he added, to ease Kate's worry.

The four of them got into a light conversation about which TV series took the prize for silliness and Emily could see Kate relaxing as they enjoyed a gourmet goulash. Having some idea of how long it had taken Alden to prepare this special dish that wasn't on the menu, Emily was sure that he and Matthew had planned the dinner earlier.

They were just discussing what dessert to order from the menu when Ben came in. He walked directly to the table and pulled up a chair without an invitation.

"Please act like you expect me," he said abruptly.

"Okay, Ben, we expect you," Matthew said.

Kate and Alden both seemed unable to say anything and they all lost interest in dessert. Ben didn't do things like this to try to be important. Something had happened.

"I sat down so that we don't get all the tongues wagging," he said. "But I need to talk to you, Kate. Will you all follow me over to the office in a few minutes?"

"We can go in my office here," Alden said, anxiously.

"And have everybody talking? No, I'll leave now. Just take a little time with dessert, then follow me."

No one retained any interest in dessert, but they managed to pretend to eat something before they deemed enough time had passed so they could leave.

The Sawtown Police Department was in a small building just down Main Street from the Blue Bird. By common consent, they walked.

Ben was sitting at his desk when they came in. He nodded toward the bench beside the door, but they all chose to stand. Alden tucked Kate inside both his arms.

"I'm sorry to keep you in suspense, Kate, but I think you need some privacy and we don't want any whisper of this to get out. Kate—" He hesitated. "You know we've been searching the forest for any sign of Jules."

Emily could see Alden's arms tighten about Kate as they waited for him to continue.

"We found a skeleton today back in Belt Ridge, inside an old cave."

He stopped again to let Kate absorb the news. "We think there's a good chance it's Jules. We searched it before when Jules first ran away, but we think he probably hid up in the Quachita mountains 'til we finally gave up."

No one spoke as they waited for him to continue. "Sheriff Carnes is taking it to Clifton for a pathology report. I know this is hard, Kate, but can you tell me if he had any dental work done?"

For a long moment, relief and something of grief struggled in Kate's face, then she buried it in Alden's shoulder and cried. No one pushed her to answer as Alden held her close, love and concern in his face. After a while she lifted her head.

"He went to Dr. Engler in Clifton. But Dr. Engler died last year." Her voice was almost a whisper.

"His records will still be available somewhere. I'll call Sheriff Carnes to check them tomorrow. But, Kate, you must realize that if this does show that Jules is dead, it won't make Julie safe. Somebody hurt her and I promise you that I'll find out who. And we'll continue to keep a guard on her until we have that person in custody."

"That's why we have to keep this just between us here," Ben added. "Not even Dave knows. Whoever is hiding behind Jules must keep thinking he's still safe."

"Ben, who besides Jules could possibly want to keep Kate and Al from marrying? Enough to use Julie as blackmail?" Matthew asked the question they were all thinking.

His voice cracking with pain, Alden said the name that was in everyone's mind, "Maxine."

"But Julie would know Maxine," Matthew objected.

"She's big enough she could disguise herself as a man and disguise her voice, too, so that a scared child wouldn't recognize it," Ben said, grimly. "I have to tell you, Alden, she is about the only suspect we have."

"No. Maxine might be willing to hurt me, but she wouldn't hurt Julie. She loves her." Kate's voice was firm.

"Nevertheless," Ben spoke in a voice no less firm, "we will know where Maxine is at all times till we know who hurt Julie. And she mustn't be left alone with her. Can you see to that, Alden?"

Alden looked like he was as much in shock as Kate, but

he nodded. "Yes. She always tells me when she's going out to see Julie. I'll go with her."

Kate managed a smile. "Bessie is acting like a mother hen, anyway. She doesn't think anyone can guard Julie like she can."

"We'll just have to see that Maxine doesn't take Julie out in the car," Alden said.

Ben nodded. "You know I'll tell you just as soon as we find out anything more," he assured Kate.

"I'm going back to the office," Kate said as soon as they were out on the sidewalk.

"Kate, you can't possibly concentrate on a stack of papers now," Emily protested. "Let them go till tomorrow."

"No. I need something to do with my hands and if I go home now, Julie can tell that something is. . .different, if she's still up. I know Bessie and Dave are with her and—"

"And Maxine's car is in front of our house," Alden finished for her.

"If you're going back there this late, we'll go with you," Matthew said. "You don't know that it's only Julie who might be in danger."

Alden nodded. "And if I talk to Maxine now, she'll guess that something is different. I'm not ready to see her yet."

Emily agreed. "And I have to sign all those triplicates you're insisting on producing." She had a strong feeling that Caroline wouldn't be one bit unhappy that she should be late getting home if Matthew Barnes was involved.

In the clinic, Kate turned on lights and went immediately to the front desk. Emily sat beside her, pen in hand. She filled in diagnoses and treatments from files Kate handed her and signed her name numerous times. They worked almost in silence while the men stood by the door and talked in low tones. Emily saw Matthew place his hand on Al's shoulder and realized that they were close enough friends that Al felt free to express his own distress now that Kate wasn't leaning on him.

Emily put her pen down and flexed her hand. "We're definitely interviewing this friend of yours as soon as you can get her in—" She stopped abruptly at a sound from Kate.

"What is it, Kate?"

Kate's face was white and stiff with shock. Something in the sound she made brought Matthew and Alden to the counter. She held a piece of dirty looking paper in her hand.

"It was stuck in this stack of papers," she gasped, holding it up toward Alden. Alden seemed paralyzed. Matthew took the paper and read it aloud.

"You are warned. Don't marry if you love Julie. She'll be hurt."

seven

"Kate." Al came alive and was around the counter holding Kate in his arms while her whole body shook with sobs.

Matthew reached across the desk for the phone and, in a few short words, explained enough to Ben to bring him on the run.

While they waited, Matthew concentrated on the note, frowning slightly. When Ben came in he handed it to him. Alden kept his arms around a quieting Kate while Ben examined the note.

"This was written on a typewriter," he said, grimly. "It can't be done by somebody hiding in the woods."

"My thoughts exactly," Matthew said.

Kate lifted her head, tears still streaking her face. "It was somebody who was in here yesterday or today. Somebody slipped it into that stack of papers."

"You have records of everyone who was in here?" Ben asked.

"To see me, yes," Emily answered him. "But a lot of the time there was nobody at the desk since we don't have a receptionist yet and Kate was back with me. Anybody could have come in and looked like they were delivering something."

Kate shuddered. "I can't stand the thought that whoever is threatening Julie is free to walk in here and leave that note."

72

"Maxine been in here?" Emily suspected that Ben sounded rough because he hated having to ask the blunt question.

"She brought Julie in to get her stitches out," Kate said. "But they came through the back door."

"No, they didn't, Kate," Emily corrected. "You let them out the back door, but we had a patient when they came and they waited out here while we finished."

Kate took in a deep breath. "Can't we just ask her, Al? It seems only fair to give her a chance to defend herself."

"No." Ben's voice was firm. "Do you really think she would admit that she's so possessive of her brother that she would be capable of wounding a child to get her way?"

"Then what do we do?" Al asked. His face showed the agony he was feeling about the sister who had cared for him.

"We do something to bring whoever it is out into the open. We don't call Maxine guilty until we know, Al, but Kate can't go on like this."

"What did you have in mind, Ben?"

Ben looked thoughtful. "How about if you let it be known that you're not going to let anyone keep you from marrying Kate? In fact, let it be known that you're setting the date up to say, this Sunday. That will give us time to check with whoever has Dr. Engler's records and know for sure that it's the skeleton of Jules that we found."

Kate pulled away from Alden, her expression a mixture of determination and horror. "You're talking about using Julie for bait. I won't do it."

"Now, Kate, you know that I won't let Julie be hurt.

We'll find a place to keep her safe till we find whoever is playing tricks on you. Maybe somewhere in Clifton."

"No. I won't let her out of my sight. Someone could find her there."

"How about letting her stay here in the clinic?" Matthew asked. "It would be easy to guard. No one's going to try to do anything to her here, anyway, with all the coming and going. And, at night, one of us could quietly stay here with her while Dave keeps watch outside."

"Sounds like a good idea to me. Kate? Al?" Ben waited a minute while Kate and Alden exchanged glances.

"I think it would work, Kate," Alden said. "We could just let everyone think that she's going home with you at night." He hesitated. "Even Maxine," he added slowly. "There's nothing would make me happier than marrying you sooner than we had planned," he added, letting his love for Kate show in his eyes as plainly as if they were alone.

Kate was silent for a minute. "All right. I know I can trust you all more than anyone in the world. Bessie will have to know, but she'll shut her tongue like a clam around Julie to protect her."

Emily hugged Kate briefly. "Kate that's the most beautiful mixed metaphor I've ever heard," she said. The brief laugh that followed eased the tension for them all.

"Now," Matthew said, "we have to set ourselves up a strict schedule for staying with Julie so she's never alone."

"We'll bring Bessie in to stay with her while the clinic's open," Emily said. "Kate, could Bessie be a sort of receptionist?"

"Of course. And Julie can sit here with her. She'll be happy with books and pictures to color. Actually, Bessie will love greeting people and having her here will really help us."

"I'll have to tell Mom something for the nights I stay with her," Emily said. "But that won't be a problem. I'll just let her think I've got someone in our observation room. That won't be lying to her."

"I think Caroline could know what we're doing," Alden said. "She'd never tell."

"That's a good idea," Ben said, briefly, but Emily thought she saw a glimmer of relief in his eyes. He seemed more at ease that they were trusting Caroline. Emily agreed with him. She didn't want any more secrets from her mother.

"Actually," she said, "I probably should stay with her every night. I'm the only one who can be here openly and no one will question. Kate has to go home if we're going to make it look like Julie is there."

After a moment of reflection, they agreed with her. Matthew announced firmly that he would be in the darkened waiting room every night.

Just before the somber group broke up, Kate asked them to pray with her. They formed a rough circle, holding hands across the desk and counter for a few minutes of silent prayer for help and support.

Then Matthew announced to Emily that he was following her home. "If you insist on staying out there in the wilderness," he said.

"Oh, Matthew, are you still bugging me about that?"

"I'll stop bugging you about that when I know that Jules

Donagan is dead," Matthew answered, grimly.

After the alarming experience earlier, Emily had to admit that it was comforting to see his lights behind her. He waited in Caroline's driveway without speaking to her, then left after she was safely inside.

Bessie turned out to be a great help to Emily and Kate on the next two days. And many of the patients told them they understood why Julie was staying there daytimes now that the invitations to Kate's wedding had gone out. There were somewhat fewer patients than they had earlier as the people of the community talked with an enjoyable thrill of the "danger of going in there."

But there was no unusual happening as Kate lived under the strain of waiting for the dental report and hurrying up the simple plans for the wedding.

"Which still may not happen," she said, looking at Julie's back as she slumped in a chair at the desk. "I'm not sure I can actually go through with it while Julie feels the way she does about it."

"When we get this mystery cleared up, she may turn back into the person she used to be," Emily said. "If not, you may need to take her for some counseling. Neither of you are going to be able to find any happiness if you let this break you and Al up. She might even resent later that you didn't marry him and give her a good father."

Emily found it hard to find the happy and outgoing child that Kate insisted Julie had been in this scowling, unresponsive, and miserably unhappy bit of humanity she saw sitting beside Bessie in the daytime or in the observation room with her at night. All attempts to break through to her were met with polite but short answers.

But their pretense that Julie went home with Kate and Bessie seemed to be working. Kate drew her car up close to the back door and Bessie, carrying a blow-up doll that Matthew had found in Clifton, scurried out. She placed the doll behind the front seat as though Julie cowered there while Dave waited in his car behind them and followed them to Bessie's home, where the procedure was followed in reverse.

It would be hard to notice the car discretely parked on the grounds of the furniture factory that overlooked the entire back of the clinic or the other car parked in front. There was a sheriff's deputy in each car. Ben openly patrolled the clinic and streets as the citizens of Sawtown expected.

Since Alden had to stay at home to keep Maxine from catching on, no one questioned Matthew's decision to stay in the darkened waiting room. Emily changed to jeans and tee shirt after the clinic closed and slept on a tiny cot next to the hospital bed in the observation room where, so far as she could tell, Julie slept well each night.

Julie seemed to enjoy the attention of being the one who was being watched in the observation room of the clinic. That was the only thing she did ever seem to enjoy, Emily thought worriedly. She had given up trying to talk to her about anything in the situation or almost anything else because of her sullen reaction.

On Friday, Ben told Kate that the dental records had identified Jules' skeleton.

"It's not official yet, but it's sure enough for the sheriff and me."

"And for a wedding," added Alden, who had come into the clinic at lunchtime with Ben. "He's already been officially declared dead."

Kate nodded, but her expression was far from that of a happy bride-to-be. "Reverend Adams has agreed that if the records showed that Jules is dead he will be happy to perform the ceremony Sunday. And Evangeline is already practicing our songs on the organ."

Emily guessed that Kate's seeming lack of any emotion was a result of the shock of the last several days. She suspected and hoped that Kate would cry out her strain in Al's arms before the day was out.

On Friday evening, Matthew brought a Monopoly game and insisted that they play in the observation room.

"I haven't played Monopoly for, well, since I was Julie's age," Emily said.

"Neither have I," Matthew answered, setting up the board on Julie's bed, "so I felt a real need to play again."

Julie and Emily sat on the side of her bed and Matthew pulled up the one chair in front of them. "I think when I played when I was Julie's age we sat on the floor, but, Julie, we can't expect a dignified doctor to sit on the floor can we?"

"We can, too," Emily answered, as a sudden movement by Julie caused the board to tilt. "But only if I can have the flat iron. I always win when I have the flat iron."

Laughing, they moved the board to the floor and all sat around it. Julie played a fierce and efficient game and won without any concessions from either Emily or Matthew.

"I always won when I had the engine," Matthew said ruefully. "I guess things change with time."

Emily wondered if he was trying to draw Julie into a conversation, but his remark made her curious, and maybe it would help if they talked about childhoods.

"You know all about how Julie and I grew here in Sawtown," she said, "but what about you? Are you a mystery man?"

"Not at all. I was an only child in Washington State. My dad was a lumber man like me. I love the forests."

A bitter remark trembled on Emily's tongue, but she bit it back. Now wasn't the time. "So you were an only child, too. We're three only children playing here on the floor."

Matthew looked intently at her, then transferred his gaze to Julie. "It's too late to change that for you and me, but Julie will probably have brothers and sisters. It's only two days 'til her mom and Al get married."

Emily barely suppressed a gasp. What a thing to say to Julie. But Matthew smiled at Julie without any sign that he might be aware of her response.

That response was immediate and devastating. Julie stood up and turned into the withdrawn child who nursed her unhappiness into an obsession. Under her anger toward Matthew, Emily felt a strong desire to shake her. After a minute or so she found she could turn her feelings into a prayer for her.

Matthew impassively gathered up the Monopoly game and told them goodnight. Emily wondered if he might be getting a touch irritable from sleeping on a not very comfortable waiting room couch for what was to be his third night.

Julie silently went into the tiny bathroom off the room and changed to pajamas, but Emily only slipped off her shoes and lay down on the cot in the jeans and tee shirt she had changed into at the end of office hours. She was tired enough to go to sleep shortly after she heard Julie's breathing slow down.

She woke suddenly and completely as she had learned to do in internship. Something was wrong. She looked at Julie's bed, seeing the mussed covers in the dim light from the barely cracked bathroom door. Julie wasn't there.

Telling herself that Julie had wakened her by going into the bathroom, Emily rose and padded to the door. The bathroom was empty.

Without taking time to slip on her shoes, she ran out to the dark waiting room. "Matthew. Matthew, where are you? I can't find Julie."

There was no answer. Flicking on her pocket flashlight, Emily played the light around the room. Matthew wasn't there either.

Heart in her mouth, Emily flicked the waiting room light on twice, waited a minute and did it again, in a prearranged signal for the watching men outside in the car. *God, don't let them be taking a nap*, she prayed.

She hurried back down the dark hall between the exam rooms, wondering if someone might be hiding in those lab and X-ray rooms she had been so proud of. Should she take the time to look in each of them?

But looking down the hall, she saw that there was a light on in the tiny kitchen in back. Wishing she had something bigger than her pocket flashlight, she ran down the hall, her stockinged feet making no sound. Maybe just her presence would help Matthew and Julie deal with whatever darkly perverted personality they were facing—if they hadn't already been forced to leave.

She stopped abruptly in the door of the kitchen, unable to believe what she saw. Matthew and Julie stood silently facing each other beside the counter, not a foot apart. Matthew held a butcher knife, point up, in his hand.

As Emily stood in shocked paralysis, a momentary picture of a bearded Matthew holding Julie by the side of the road blocked out the unbelievable scene in front of her. How could Matthew have played such a game with them all, pretending he was still a close friend to Alden, that love for Kate hadn't turned him into a maddened monster who was willing to do anything to prevent her marriage? How could even Ben have been fooled? Because Matthew used a pretended interest in herself to cover his secret?

She looked around for something, anything, to use as a weapon, but the only possible weapons in the room were in drawers beside Matthew and Julie. She opened her mouth to scream. Maybe just knowing that she was there would keep Matthew from carrying out whatever he planned to do.

Then, before she could do anything, Julie suddenly moved forward and collapsed, sobbing, against Matthew.

"Oh, Matthew, I couldn't do it. I wanted to just cut myself a little so Mom wouldn't marry and leave me, but I— it hurt too much before."

Emily stood clinging to the door jamb for support as

Matthew dropped the knife on the counter and held Julie tenderly.

"Julie, what happened the first time, when I found you in the woods?"

"I fell." Julie took in a shuddering breath. "I was running in the yard and I fell on something," she said between sobs. "It hurt and I was going to go tell Bessie, then, I thought. . .if I said my dad did it, maybe I could keep Mom from marrying Al, like Maxine said I should. . .so I went in the woods and. . .I wasn't really lost when you found me. . .I heard you tell Al where you were going. . ."

One of the deputies came running down the hall, then stopped in perplexity when Emily put her finger to her mouth. Matthew and Julie didn't look up from their intense discussion. Emily whispered to him to go watch for Ben and the other deputy and tell them everything was all right. Reluctantly, the deputy left.

Matthew lifted Julie up to the counter, so that their eyes were on a level. "Julie, now tell me why you thought your mom would leave you when she married. You know she and Al love you and want to be a family with you."

"Maxine said. . .she said I mustn't tell anyone. . .she told me...that Mom and Al would shove me out. . .just like they were shoving her out. . .and if I didn't want to be shoved out. . .I'd better tell Mom she couldn't marry him . . .and when I hurt myself I thought. . ."

Julie stopped and leaned forward against Matthew's chest, crying like the child she was, for the first time since Emily had known her. He held her quietly, letting her cry it out, but the cold anger in his eyes showed his emotions. He looked up and saw Emily and his expression softened as he met her eyes. He held Julie a little more tightly, seeming to struggle with his own emotions.

Then he took her by her shoulders and made her meet his eyes again. "Julie, we've all learned in church that we don't judge anyone and, as you finish growing up in a family with Kate and Al, and you remember Maxine, you will want to just say a prayer for her. But, for now, I'm sure Kate won't want you to spend any more time with her and you must understand that she hasn't been thinking right about Kate and Al's love for you. She was putting her own unhappiness on you. You know how much your mother loves you, don't you?"

Julie nodded.

"And do you understand now that she would never push you out of her life? She wouldn't marry Al if Al didn't love you and want you all to be a family, too. Do you believe me, Julie?" He curved his hands about Julie's face and looked intently at her.

Julie nodded again.

"All right, Julie. Now we're going to call your mother and tell her to go ahead with those wedding plans and you want to be part of it. All right?"

For the first time Julie smiled. "I read about giving the bride away in a book," she said shyly. "Do you suppose I could give her to Al? But I wouldn't really give her away."

"I think," Matthew said, lifting Julie down to the floor, "that would make your mom know better than anything else that you understand how much she and Al love you."

Emily slipped into her office so that Julie wouldn't have

to deal with seeing her as she and Matthew went out to the reception desk to call Kate. She stayed there, working on her charts and ignoring the time, until the happy sounds from the front told her Kate and Al had come to pick up Julie. The silence in the clinic made her believe that she was alone.

"Time to go home, Doc." Matthew stood in the doorway of her office, looking as tired and, at the same time, as exhilarated as she felt.

"Matthew, those things you said when we were playing Monopoly. . .you knew Julie was making it all up, didn't you? Did you know that she left the letter on Kate's desk herself?"

"I guessed. Especially after Ben told us that the dental records showed that Jules died in that cave. The only two people who could be against Kate and Al getting married were Maxine and Julie and, frightened of losing Al as Maxine was, I couldn't see her actually hurting Julie. Julie's attitude toward the marriage has changed so much recently that it seemed sure Maxine was working on her emotions. And that day I found Julie in the woods, I felt like something was wrong in what she told me, but I couldn't put my finger on it. Yesterday, I realized she should have been hysterical if what she said had really happened and she wasn't."

"Did she wake you up when she went down to the kitchen? I slept right through it," Emily admitted with a rueful grin.

Matthew groaned. "I sat in one of the desk chairs so I could watch. Those chairs are not relaxers."

Emily laughed, then sobered. "As you told Julie, it's not

our place to judge, but I keep asking myself how Maxine could do that to a child?"

"She probably didn't realize what she was causing. Maybe just thought if Julie threw a tantrum Kate would give in."

"You didn't tell her that her father is dead."

"No, that's something her mother will do. Now, can I drive you home, Doc?"

Emily looked outside. "Matthew, it's getting light. I've got patients coming."

"Fine. You can nap on the way home. I'm sure you'll feel more like seeing those patients if you have a quick shower and change."

Emily considered. "That sounds good. And I'm sure Mom will be happy to fix us a super breakfast before she goes to work."

Matthew grinned. "I was counting on that," he said.

eight

Dear Ryan,

I'm sure you're busy getting settled in and enjoying how much you're needed there and how much you can do for the people's health and to bring those who don't know Jesus to Him, and that's why I haven't had a letter from you. Lucky you knew your address before you left so I can write you.

My practice here started out with a real bang. I've seen more people than I used to think lived in this part of Arkansas, but I know that there are people back on the side roads that haven't seen a doctor in, well, who knows how long? I think about the babies and little children who don't get their immunization shots and wish I could do something about it.

I told you last week a little about my nurse, Kate. Have you had time to read it yet? It was almost like a detective story. She was to marry and her husband, (he's her husband now, so you can guess that the story had a happy ending) Al's sister got so in control of Julie's (that's Kate's daughter)

*emotions that Julie tried to hurt herself to
keep them from marrying.*

   *Maxine (that's the sister) was much older
than Al and raised him and she couldn't
stand the thought of giving him up and made
Julie think (she doesn't think it anymore) that
Kate would push her out of her life.*

   Well, Matthew Barnes

Emily stopped typing. She leaned her elbows on the desk
in her room and gazed out the window into the front yard,
not really seeing the cardinal bringing a last evening snack
to her babies in the bush outside her window. Should she
mention Matthew to Ryan? Somehow, she didn't want to.
She cleared out his name and started the sentence over.

   *Well, we had some days of excitement, but
the wedding was beautiful. At least half the
population of Sawtown crowded into the
church to see Julie "give away" her mother,
and enjoy the great food at the reception.*

   *Anyway, they're deliriously happy and
Maxine has gone back to Boston to live. She
said she had no idea that she would cause
Julie to try to hurt herself and we do believe
her. And, just to prove that we are not
capable of and shouldn't try to judge anyone
else, it turns out she is the anonymous donor
of all the extras in the clinic that I told you
about earlier. (I do hope you're getting my*

letters.)

Al knew that Maxine was our "angel" but she had made him promise not to tell. When the bad things about her came out, he decided to break his promise and tell the good things. He still loves his sister and appreciates what she's done for him.

Anyway, it seems that she did some very smart investments and really has quite a lot of money, so she won't have a problem with that. And we just pray that she will be able to find a life of her own now (as well as another restaurant of her own).

Kate is taking Julie to Clifton to a Christian counselor there, but we think she won't need much now that she accepts that she's loved.

We have a really sharp secretary/receptionist named Cammie Johnson. She's young but she's worked in a doctor's office in Clifton, so she isn't going to find it hard to catch on to our needs. Kate is waiting until she gets her trained to take a honeymoon.

Surprise Number 2. Mom and Ben McGowan, the police chief of Sawtown, are

Emily stopped again. She leaned back in her chair and took a drink of iced cappuccino coffee from a glass beside the typewriter. She held it in her mouth for awhile, deliberately concentrating on the rich chocolatey smoothness of the coffee instead of the words she was trying to get on her paper.

Papa cardinal flew in, letting Emily turn her attention to his bright feathers as he perched on a branch and checked out the neighborhood for safety before going about his fatherly duties of helping to fill up his children's stomachs.

Father. It was ridiculous to feel like Caroline Richards was being unfaithful to a memory. Yet she did.

She thought of a discussion with Matthew a few days ago. Matthew had come to the booth in the Blue Bird where she was unwinding with a soft drink after a busy day. The conversation, general at first, soon turned to the subject of Caroline and Ben. Emily suspected him of deliberately steering it that way and let her resentment show in a snapping refusal to discuss them.

"Emily Richards, MD, you can't keep on clinging to being Daddy's little girl forever, you know," he replied.

Emily gasped. "How can you say I'm being Daddy's little girl forever? I've never been Daddy's little girl, except for a dim memory. The forest took him from me. No, not the forest. The forest is kind. The men killing the forest killed him."

Matthew sounded irritated. "The forest is neither kind nor cruel. It just is. You can love it or hate it, but you can't make it have emotions. But I believe God meant for us to use it with the intelligence He gave us."

"My father was being forced to clear cut to make a living, and I know how much he loved the forest. I really believe that if he could tell us now, he would say the forest was justified in taking revenge."

"Emily, that's pagan. I love the forest, as your father did, but I don't give it intelligence. A tree falls as it falls. The accident that killed your father was probably caused by human error. And," he sounded like he was speaking to Julie, "you certainly aren't justified in taking out your feelings about your father against your mother."

"Why, Matthew, how can you say that? I know what Mom has done for me. I appreciate her. I love her."

"But you don't give her the right to make decisions about her life. You don't give her the right to happiness with someone else. That hurts the ideal marriage you carry in your mind that she had with your father."

Father. Emily deliberately turned away from the bright red bird swinging on his branch. Though she had left Matthew in anger, she was now almost ready to admit to herself that he was at least partly right. Her mother deserved to have someone with her, loving her, for the rest of her life.

Could he be right, too, when he'd said that Caroline wasn't talking about her feelings for Ben because she had picked up Emily's negative reactions and wanted to wait until she was well settled into her new practice in Sawtown before she brought it up?

With a sudden decision, Emily put down her glass and left her letter to Ryan unfinished. Caroline certainly shouldn't have to deal with an adult child who was reverting to childhood now. Then she picked up her coffee and went to find Caroline.

Caroline was sitting on the patio, wearing a pair of old jeans with dirt from her garden on the knees. She was looking off into the trees and didn't seem to hear Emily come out.

"Mom?" Emily spoke softly, somehow reluctant to bring Caroline back from whatever memories she must be living in.

"S-s-h," Caroline softly. "There's a red fox out there. Just inside the edge of the trees. I think she's raising babies there, but I've never been able to see them."

Emily realized that her mother wasn't living in the past at all. Caroline was getting all the enjoyment out of the present. This moment. What a healthy way to live. With an inward grimace, Emily reminded herself she could still take a few lessons from her mom.

"Oh, Mom," she teased. "Last night it was a friendly skunk. And you wouldn't even let me scream when it came up to the patio. You've turned into a Dr. Doolittle since I've been gone."

"I know." Caroline smiled happily, then turned solemn. Emily didn't ask her what flitting thought brought the slight frown to her forehead.

"I'll move very quietly so I don't scare Mama Fox and get you a glass of cappuccino. Or would you rather have iced tea?"

"Tea, please." Caroline smiled at her, then turned her attention back to the trees.

Emily went into the kitchen and filled a glass with ice, then poured tea from the pitcher which was always in Caroline's refrigerator. She refilled her own glass with coffee and carried them both out to the patio. She set the tea on a table beside Caroline's chair, than sank into a high-backed woven chair beside her. Then she jerked upright.

"Oh, no. There's the skunk again."

Caroline smiled. "And the fox seems to be gone. It just amazes me, Emily, how she can just fade away even while I think I'm watching her."

Emily laughed. "I see you're ignoring the little black-and-white kitty. Oh, look, there's two of them."

"He's just a friendly little baby," Caroline said. "And that's probably his sister taking an evening stroll with him. The mama is undoubtedly somewhere around."

Emily took a drink of coffee. "You'd miss this place tremendously if you ever left here, wouldn't you?"

Caroline turned to her in surprise. "Why do you ask that?"

"I. . . Look, Mom, it's not hard to see that you and Ben have some feelings for each other."

"Look, they're playing like a couple of kittens." Caroline kept her gaze on the two skunks who were rolling together near the flower bed. Then she turned to face Emily squarely.

"I've been trying to get myself to talk to you about Ben," she said.

"Well, do it now," Emily answered softly.

"Emily, I tried to keep the memory of your father alive while I was raising you and I missed him tremendously. I didn't have time to think about marrying again. Good friends in the church made it easier for me. As you must remember, Ben and Shirley were among the best of our friends. And, of course, there was nothing between us then. Ben was happily married. But after Shirley died three years ago, he started coming in to the Blue Bird to eat and we talked and. . ." She took in a deep breath. "He wants us to be married, Emily."

Emily jumped and jerked her feet up to the edge of her chair. "Mom, they're up here with us."

Caroline looked at the two curious skunks squatting on the patio in front of them and chortled. "Just don't scare them, Emily."

Emily carefully put her feet down flat on the floor. "Is it all right to talk?" she whispered.

"If you really want to." Caroline's face showed that she wasn't referring to the skunk situation.

Emily looked at her mother and answered frankly. "I grew up in this yard. I've seen foxes and skunks before. Maybe I'm sort of. . .hiding behind them? Do you think?"

"You might be."

Moving carefully, Emily reached out for Caroline's hand. "Mom, I want you to know that I want happiness for you."

"That's a long way from saying you want me to marry Ben," Caroline said bluntly.

From somewhere out near the trees a warning twitter sounded and the two babies scurried off. Silently Emily and Caroline watched them go.

"I do want you to marry Ben if that's what will make you happy. Any problem I have with Daddy's memory is my problem, not yours."

"Emily, I loved your father and would have spent the rest of my life with him if God had chosen to let me do that. Ben felt the same way about Shirley. Marrying each other would have nothing to do with memories of them. We know that there is a time when we accept what is and move on. I did that long ago. But, I think now that I tried so hard to make you feel like you knew your father and appreciate the good man that he was that I planted emotions in you that had no base in reality."

"Reality was that he was killed making money for the lumber company and that you were given such a small amount of their money that you had to work in the Blue Bird forever. Did you forgive them for that?"

"What they gave me I saved for your education and I would have saved it no matter how much it was. Yes, I long ago forgave everyone connected with the accident. And I enjoy working in the Blue Bird, Emily."

Emily looked out to the dimming trees. The little skunks were nowhere in sight. "It's safe to move now." She went over and knelt before her mother, sliding her arms about her waist and dropping her head to Caroline's lap the way she did when she was eight.

"Mom, I don't think I ever tell you enough how much I thank you for being my mother and how much I love you."

Caroline leaned forward and kissed Emily's head. "Yes, you do. I know." She sounded so calmly sure of herself that Emily knew she did know. But how would she feel when Emily told her she felt like she was meant to go to the medical mission field?

Emily didn't want to raise her head and meet her eyes. *God*, she asked silently, *am I sure of Your plans for me? But You sometimes require us to leave our families even if they don't understand. Remember, Jesus had to follow His duty even when it hurt His family.*

She slowly raised her head. "Mom," she started.

But Caroline didn't seem to hear her. She was looking toward the now dark woods. "I do want to marry Ben, honey, but I've lived here so long I don't want to leave it. He has a nice house in town and," she laughed a little, "goodness knows town isn't all that big, but. . ."

Emily breathed a sigh of relief that she had been kept from confiding her plans. *Some other time will be better*, she thought. *Now we need to talk about her plans.* And a sudden idea nestled into her head as if it had been there for eons.

"Mom, his house in town is just about right for me. It's so near the clinic and I get called out at night more than he does. Why don't I rent it and you and Ben live out here?"

It was too dark now to read Caroline's expression but Emily felt, more than heard, her quickly suppressed gasp and knew it was relief. She realized that even her own coming home, much as her mother had looked forward to it, had been a block to Caroline planning for her own needs after so many years.

Caroline's voice was carefully casual. "I'll talk to Ben. He might agree."

Emily rose and gave her mom a quick kiss, determined to leave her alone with her happy thoughts. "I'm going in. I was in the middle of a letter." She stopped at the door. "But, you know this is true, Mom. The skunks never came up on the patio in all the years I was growing up here."

"We were just lucky tonight, baby," Caroline answered calmly.

nine

Dear Emily,

It is unbelievably chaotic here but there is one person, a nurse, who knows all the ins and outs of everybody's jobs and makes it possible to get something accomplished. She has learned the language the way the people speak it and when I find my book jargon doesn't work, she runs interference for me. She is really a great person who lives her Christianity every day.

Someone brought in a child, two or three years old, it's hard to tell ages of these children, they are all so old in suffering. Anyway this little guy was so dehydrated and so close to death, we thought we wouldn't be able to save him. But we did, Emily. We saved him. You know how we used to feel when we pulled off a miracle in St. Louis? Well, it's twice that feeling here, because in St. Louis if I hadn't been there, someone else would. I'm not sure that's true here.

There are a million stories here to tell you but I'm dead on my feet, so, till later. . .

Still looking forward to having you

here with me.

Love,
Ryan

Emily read Ryan's letter hurriedly, in her office between patients, then put it carefully away from her stack of patient files to read again later. *When I get the time*, she thought ruefully. Time seemed to be something she had lost.

But she considered that she had gained a lot. She had been able to put her feelings about her father's death in some kind of vault inside herself so she could be honestly happy for Caroline and Ben. In fact, one reason she had so little time now was that she needed to get everything cleared away for their wedding rehearsal.

Thank goodness it's Friday, she thought. *Only a half day tomorrow if I'm lucky, and I'll have time to help Mom get ready. I wonder if she's the slightest bit nervous. She certainly doesn't show it if she is. She seems so sure of herself. And she and Ben are so openly happy. Just like Kate and Al.*

Could I be just a little bit jealous? It seems like I'm walking around the edges of a deliriously happy pink world that belongs to other people. And I can't even wear Ryan's ring until I can get a promise from Joyce or another doctor to come to Sawtown and even then it's two years. No, a year and ten months.

"Emily Richards, stop feeling sorry for yourself," she whispered. "You're a lucky person to be doing what you want to do even if it isn't where you want to do it. So get out there and do it."

She pushed a fleeting thought of Matthew Barnes out of her mind as she walked down the short hall to the exam room. Then she smiled. She did like him. And Caroline's and Kate's attempts to throw them together were kind of cute.

She felt a spontaneous little smile playing around her mouth the rest of the day while she listened to symptoms of adults and cajoled children into letting her look in their throats and ears. She was through in plenty of time for the wedding rehearsal.

Emily kept Saturday morning hours in the clinic for those parents in the community and surrounding countryside who worked and could only bring their children in then. Very often she was still there late in the afternoon. But on the hot July Saturday of Caroline's wedding, she and Kate looked out on an empty waiting room at eleven o'clock.

"Everyone is home getting ready for the wedding," Kate said. "No child would dare to be sick today."

"Well," Emily said, smiling. "Let's leave right now."

Caroline and Ben had compromised between their desire to have a simple ceremony and their knowledge that everyone would want to be there by putting a general invitation in the church bulletin and hanging one up on the door of the Blue Bird.

When Emily got to the house by the woods, where Ben's favorite pieces of furniture had already been placed, she found Caroline still so in control that she needed little help. Both of their dresses were pressed and hanging, ready to slip into for the four o'clock ceremony.

Emily made small cottage cheese salads and poured iced

tea. She took them and a basket of crackers out to the patio table. Then she called Caroline, who came out in a brightly colored caftan.

"I wouldn't be half so sure of myself if I didn't know that I'm coming back to this house," she said in response to Emily's remark about her super cool. "When Ben agreed to your idea about you renting his house and us living here, the last piece fell in place. I can't thank you enough, Emily. For that and for understanding about your father."

Emily smiled and pretended to be absorbed in the busy life of the yard. Now she had two private problems that she couldn't be totally open about to her mother. Added to her desire to go to the mission field was the fact that her feelings about her father had only been put away, not resolved.

But she caught her mother's hand and assured her, truthfully, of her complete acceptance of her happiness with Ben.

Later, waiting in the lobby of the crowded church with Caroline, she impulsively hugged her and repeated her assurances.

Caroline wore a beige lace dress with rose encrusted scallops around the shallow scooped neck and at the wrists of the gracefully draped full sleeves. The straight line skimmed her waist to end just below the knees. A floppy straw hat in pale rose finished her ensemble. Her only ornamentation was Ben's gift of a single strand of pearls and the bouquet of wildflowers she carried.

The altar, where the Reverend Ethan Adams waited beside Matthew and Ben, was banked with baskets of wildflowers. Tiny, ribbon tied, wild roses were fastened to the ends of the pews, and garlands of white roses and verbena looped across the windows. Everything in the church reflected Caroline's love of nature.

Angeline Adams, her plump face shining with happiness for these two people she had known for so many years, played soft music on the organ as the townspeople crowded into the uncushioned pews.

Emily gave Caroline a last quick hug. Her full-skirted rose dress matched the trim on Caroline's. Her bouquet of pink roses from Caroline's garden hid the clenched hand that clutched Ben's ring. As she started up the aisle in response to Angeline's musical signal, the quiet crowd seemed to drift off into space, and she was disconcertingly aware of nothing but Matthew's gaze on her.

From his place beside Ben, Matthew watched Emily hug her mother. She did so carefully, he noted with amusement, her small body pushed away with only her shoulders touching Caroline. A female instinct, he supposed, to keep from mussing anything.

When Emily started down the aisle, he found himself able to look only at her. Some uncontrollable imp in his mind changed the flowers in her hand to a shepherdess' crook. It laced white ribbons across the bodice of her dress and added checks to the full skirt to make her the picture in his childhood picture book. Then the little imp lengthened her full-skirted gown to the tips of her shoes and turned the rose to white. Suddenly he saw her smiling face through the pale mist of a white veil.

Just before she reached the altar and stood opposite him,

he blinked her back into the becoming dress and hat she was actually wearing. Shaken, he turned his attention to the bride and groom, who looked much calmer than he felt.

After the simple ceremony, the two couples rode in Ben's car to his house just off the main street, where a reception had been planned.

Ben and Caroline left the next day for a honeymoon in an unknown destination, and Emily planned to move into Ben's house while they were away.

"When are you going to move?" Kate asked on the Monday following the wedding. "I'll help."

They were having coffee in the kitchen during an unusually slow Monday morning following the wedding.

"Everyone must be too tired from the wedding to see the doctor," Cammie had commented earlier.

"Oh, Saturday afternoon. I'll do my packing slowly through the week. There isn't much to move really. Just the desk and bedroom furniture. But I'll have to find a pickup somewhere."

"Matthew might have one you can use. In fact," Kate grinned mischievously, "he might be very willing to drive it for you."

Emily grimaced. "Why do I get a feeling that we're being matchmade?" she asked with a touch of asperity.

Kate looked at her in surprise. "Because everyone thinks you and Matthew would be a perfect match," she answered, seriously.

Cammie nodded. "I heard a few remarks made at the wedding about who would be the next couple up there."

Emily sat in a strained silence. Now was the time to tell them about Ryan. Yet if she did and told them where he was, it would almost be telling them how short her stay in Sawtown was to be and she wasn't ready to do that yet.

It was a distressful situation which made her feel as if she were being hypocritical. *Yet*, she thought, *surely I wouldn't be so interested in going into the missionary field if that isn't where God meant me to be. Sawtown is just a place to wait till He and I bring another doctor in and I can fulfill His command to "go ye into all the world."*

She changed the subject so abruptly that Kate and Cammie couldn't continue discussion of any future relationship between herself and Matthew.

☙

There was more to moving out of the house where she had spent her childhood than she had indicated to Kate and Cammie. Caroline had kept all the treasures and mementos of her childhood and Emily determined to take this opportunity to go through them and discard what was no longer meaningful.

Monday evening, after a tuna salad sandwich, she changed to jeans and an untucked, old white shirt. She went into her room, determined to tackle those mementos. A beat-up old army trunk that she had always imagined belonged to her father in the Vietnam War had stood as long as she could remember in the corner of her old room. Caroline had carefully moved it when she changed rooms with her. Emily sat cross legged in front of it, a big paper sack for trash beside her.

It had always opened with a satisfying creak that, in her

childhood, gave Emily the feeling of secret and important things that only she could access. The sound of it now put her in an nostalgic mood before she had even started taking articles out.

Over in a corner almost covered by old newsletters was a high school yearbook. Stiff bits of darkened red petals fell out as she lifted it. It opened without her help at the place where a corsage had been pressed. Emily looked at the squashed stems held together by a still blue ribbon and laughed.

Tom Yates. They had dated for a year or more and she had cried for almost a month when they broke up. A few days ago, Emily had just examined his wife, who was pregnant with their third child. She would probably be her first delivery in the hospital at Clifton.

She dropped the self-destructing corsage in the sack beside her and closed the book without reading anything. It was all too long ago to be of interest now. Maybe it would become interesting again when she was older.

Several school papers that Caroline had insisted on her keeping followed the corsage into the sack. She picked up and examined some interestingly shaped rocks and two filled with fossils. She remembered where she had found each of them and carefully put them back. She lovingly rubbed the cover of the tiny New Testament that she had been given in Sunday school.

Next was a box filled with her father's medals and memorabilia from Vietnam. She knew them all intimately. She had spent hours on rainy afternoons in her childhood pouring over them. She took each of them out now, letting her mind mull over the ironic fact that he had survived the war with only a thigh wound that sent him home with a honorable discharge and had died in the battlefield that was a sawmilling outfit a few years later.

The medals were few: a rifleman, good conduct, and Purple Heart. Her father had been a man who was willing to fight the guns in Vietnam and the prejudice back in the states. A man who then replaced the violent and exotic places he had found in the world with the narrow but happy life on the edge of Sawtown with Caroline—with Caroline and a daughter who wanted desperately to remember him as more than a misty impression.

Maybe, she thought, staring at the slice of dulling sky she could see from her position on the floor, *if I could remember him, have just one flash of clear memory, I could put him where he should be in my mind*.

She replaced the medals in the box and closed it, laying it to the side where she was putting the things she wanted to keep. She was about to close the trunk when a cracked Christmas ball caught her eye.

It was real glass, one of the few good ornaments they had during the years she was growing up. An elegant handpainted blue star shot rays out of its five sharp points to meet in the back. She had never tired of listening to its story while she and Caroline decorated the small pine they took from the forest every year.

Emily could hear Caroline's voice now as she had every year. "This one was hand-blown in Scotland, Emily. And hand-painted too. It's clouded over some now because it's so old. It was clear as crystal when it was new. Your grand-

mother (too many greats back for you to be able to understand) brought it over when she emigrated to Virginia on a
sailing ship. Can you imagine how carefully she packed it
in wool to keep it from getting broken on the way over?
Then it rode in covered wagons from Virginia to Tennes-
see to Arkansas just as carefully packed so we can enjoy it
now."

Holding the ball in both hands now, Emily tried not to
remember the pain, sharp as the points of the star, of the
Christmas she had broken the ball. She was twelve that
year, old enough to stay alone during Christmas vacation
while her mother worked. To give herself something happy
to do she had brought in their decorations from the outside
store room and decided to clean the glass ball so it would
be as clear again as it had been when it was new.

In the kitchen of the Blue Bird with her mother, she had
watched them use the hottest water and strongest deter-
gent to keep everything spotlessly clean, so that was what
she determined to use for the ball. She filled a large pan
with hot water and heated it to a fast boil, then moved it to
the sink and quickly squirted soap in. She folded a small
tea towel to make a soft pad in the pan for the beloved ball.
She was still careful not to drop it as she slid it gently into
the pan.

The panic she felt at the horrible cracking sound and
flash of a zigzag crack across the star was a hurting pressure inside her that she would never forget.

Caroline was comforting when she called her on the phone
and sobbed out what she had done. She even had tried to
tell Emily that it was still beautiful and they could hang it

on the tree. But for years the sight of it made Emily so unhappy that she had asked her mother to wrap it in cotton and let her place it in with her keepsakes. She treasured some idea that there was a glue in the world or would be sometime that would erase the crack.

She watched a drop of water splash on the star as she cradled it in her hands and almost believed for a minute that perhaps the miracle that she used to hope for was happening. Then, through a dreamy mist, she recognized her own tears dripping on it.

Those tears were no longer of grief for the breaking of the ornament but of love for Caroline and all the things she had done for her.

She rewrapped the ornament and placed it back in its box, then closed the trunk on all the things, she wanted to keep, foolish or not. And she promised herself that next Christmas she would bring the cracked ornament out for Caroline's and Ben's first tree.

By Saturday afternoon she had everything packed and ready when Matthew drove up in a pick-up used by the maintenance man at the factory. Kate and Alden were behind him.

ten

It only took a short while to load the desk and bedroom furniture that Emily wanted to take with her. She locked the doors, then went back to check them again.

Matthew smiled indulgently at her. "You know, you're not leaving your childhood home to travel thousands of miles. You're only moving into town."

Emily understood that he showed a surprising sensibility to her feelings, but his choice of words brought out the nagging sense of guilt for her lack of candor in not telling even the people closest to her of her eventual plans. Still, she comforted herself, telling them now before she located another doctor for sure would only upset them.

At Ben's house she directed Al and Matthew in the placement of her desk in a small room at the front of the house that had been a family room when Ben's wife lived. Now she planned to make it into an office where she could see some patients after hours without having to open the clinic.

She had chosen a large back bedroom for her own, leaving a smaller one for a guest room. She left her clothes and personal things on the bed in that room, preferring to place them later when she was alone.

Becoming aware that she was alone in the room and she didn't hear any of the others, she went out to the kitchen to see if she could find soft drinks to offer. Kate was there, putting together a huge salad while Al and Matthew were out on the patio preparing to grill small steaks.

"We knew you probably didn't eat lunch because you would want to leave your mom's kitchen spotless," Kate explained, "so we decided to fix lunch right here."

"How thoughtful," Emily said. "Ben said he was leaving all his cooking utensils. I suspect that's probably a skillet and teakettle."

"Come look around. I don't think he ever got rid of Shirley's things. But you may want to replace some of them."

The kitchen was well stocked with utensils and Emily decided that she could wait until later to buy things as she might need them. "I'm not the world's greatest cook, anyway," she said out loud.

"Me neither," Kate admitted cheerfully. "Thank goodness Al is, or we all might starve. Bessie fed Julie so much that I didn't worry about it then. She still does when Al and I are both working and she keeps her."

"Julie has turned into a whole other person in my eyes," Emily spoke tentatively.

"You're just now seeing the real Julie. The one you saw when you first came was created by Maxine. I have to keep forgiving myself over and over for not realizing that soon enough."

"And Maxine?" Emily busied herself picking out silverware and looking for steak knives, to give Kate a chance not to answer if she chose.

"Julie and I still see Dr. Sevier once in awhile, but we're about to grow out of our need for him. At bedtime some nights we pray together with Al for Maxine. And, we're not sure yet that Maxine's being totally honest with us, but her letters sound like she's fairly content. It's going to be all right."

"That sounds super good." Emily pulled out steak knives from the back of a drawer and washed them quickly at the sink. "Oh, Matthew and Al seem to either be fighting off smoke or waving to us to come out."

"The last I hope," Kate said. "Salad's ready, too. Lucky I thought to bring oil and vinegar." She picked up the bowl and Emily followed her out with plates, napkins, and silverware.

"They're perfect," Matthew announced, taking the plates out of Emily's hand and placing them about the umbrella topped table. He deftly slipped a steak on each plate while Kate set the salad on the table and went back in for a jug of iced tea. They settled down to enjoying the delicious meal.

"Mmm," Emily said, savoring every bite, "I didn't realize how hungry I was."

"Well, just in case you find yourself terribly hungry and there's no one here to cook for you and you don't want to cook for yourself, just remember that you're in walking distance of the Blue Bird," Al announced.

Emily wondered briefly if the convoluted sentence meant Al had entered the game of "let's match Emily and Matthew."

Matthew may have thought the same thing, for he simply pointed out that everyone in town was in walking distance of the Blue Bird.

"Yeah," Al answered smugly, "that's why we sometimes

call it the Blue Bird of Happiness."

They all laughed and took the conversation into a light discussion of the problem of mowing the back lawn, which sloped off rather sharply into a tiny stream bed, now dry in the summer heat. Emily relaxed and let herself enjoy the meal and her friends.

"That little stream reminds me that I need, I really need, to go on a canoe trip," Kate said firmly. "I haven't been since the three of us and Julie went last year. Remember how grown-up Julie felt riding 'shotgun' in the canoe with you, Matthew? This time we'll have to be a family in one canoe and you and Emily can ride in the other. And we'll swim and eat lunch on a sandbar."

Kate stopped for a minute, maybe aware that, in her enthusiasm, she was openly making plans to throw Matthew and Emily together. "You do like canoeing, don't you, Emily?" she asked.

"I used to love it," Emily answered, truthfully. "But it's been a long time. I'm not sure I remember how to paddle."

"Of course you do," Al said. "It's like—well, like rowing a boat. Once you learn you never forget. And this year," he teased Kate, grinning, "now that we're married, I plan to lean back and let you do all the rowing."

Kate threw her napkin at him. "Dream on, muscle man. But really, do we want to make plans now?"

"How about two weeks from today?" Matthew suggested. "That would give Emily next Saturday to do all the things she needs to in her new home. But I do warn you, Emily, that Julie swung a terrific paddle. You'll have to really work to come up to her speed."

"Sure," Kate guffawed. "How many times did she almost tip you over with her terrific paddle?"

"A few," Matthew admitted, grinning.

They spent several minutes remembering and laughing about their float trip. Emily sat quietly, enjoying their camaraderie and feeling a part of it, even though she hadn't been a part of the experience. She felt warmed by their friendship and by Matthew's thoughtfulness in giving her a weekend alone to settle into the house.

Before they cleared up the lunch dishes and left, they agreed on a Saturday date in late July.

＆

Dear Emily,

I'm sorry I'm not writing more often. It is unbelievably chaotic here. But there is one person, a nurse, who knows all the ins and outs and makes it possible for everybody to do his job. I may have mentioned her before. ("You did," Emily muttered. "You certainly did.") She only got her nursing degree and came out here three years ago herself, but she manages us all beautifully and is loved by the children, even when she's giving them immunization shots. We're really going all out on that now. Our goal is to get every child under six inoculated in the next year. Big hopes, but I really believe we can do it.

Wish I could see you. . .here.

Hurriedly,

Love,

Ryan

Emily put Ryan's letter down on the patio table, where she had been reading it while eating her chicken salad supper. She looked at it thoughtfully, admitting her disappointment to herself.

She had expected long, intimate letters giving anecdotes and details of his life in the field. She hadn't received one that was more than one page long, and he always skimmed over his activities without giving her any idea of what actually went on there.

Telling herself that Ryan might just be one of those people who weren't good letter writers, who were better at doing than writing about it, she gathered the letter up with the rest of her mail and carried it in to her desk. In spite of its shortness, there was something in the letter that made her thoughtful. Was he doing more immunization in Africa than she was doing in Arkansas?

She brought the subject up the next day during a hurried lunch in the clinic kitchen.

"Kate, we're starting immunizations with the babies we're seeing, but I haven't seen some of them back for the rest of the series."

"I know," Kate answered. "A lot of them won't be back. Some of them can't afford it, at least not until they're ready for school and have to."

"But what about between now and school age?"

"It just isn't done. They can go in to the public health clinic in Clifton, but they have to wait there and it takes several hours and the mothers just don't take them. Most of the mothers work. A lot of them work at Matthew's furniture place."

"Then that's how we'll do it."

"Do what?"

"Have our own immunization clinic. We'll do it for the cost of the serum."

Kate's eyes sparkled. "I'm following you. We'll get Matthew to have some kind of Family Day and get all his employees' kids done. Then we'll work on the others."

"And maybe I can get Jane Smith to come down and do mammograms for the women at the same time. Last time I was in Clifton I stopped off at the radiology department and talked to her about it. She said she'd come if we set up something on her day off."

"Let's start working on it now. We can plan it with Matthew during the canoe trip this Saturday."

Emily hesitated. "We're taking it for granted that Matthew will agree," she said. "Maybe he won't."

"Of course he will. Matthew Barnes would do it just for the good of Sawtown. But sometime you are going to have to notice that he will do almost anything for you."

Kate put down her coffee cup. "I'll get patients into the exam rooms for you." She left without giving Emily a chance to react.

Emily finished her coffee thoughtfully. Could they really expect Matthew to agree to lose a day's work at the factory?

They could, she discovered, as they were driving down to Cricket Creek on Saturday afternoon in Matthew's car while an animated Julie sat between Al and Kate in the back seat. Comfortably dressed in white shorts and a red tee shirt over her swim suit, Emily was glad she could lean against the front door away from Matthew.

She watched the vista open up to occasional fields of corn drooping in the July heat or narrow down as trees or stone bluffs leaned over the curving road. She felt somehow more secure being able to get farther away from Matthew's space-shrinking presence while he was driving than she could if they were in the back seat.

Now she relaxed and let her mind drift from one pleasant thought to another without really listening to the desultory conversation going on in the car.

She was brought back by a sudden realization that there was a silence in the car. Matthew was looking at her with an affectionate smile that startled her. She quickly looked down, not sure how to respond to the kind of an indulgent look that a father might have for a child. Or a man for his sweetheart. The thought went through her mind, unbidden.

"She's dreaming, I think," he said.

"But, Emily," Kate called, "I'm talking about making one of your dreams come true."

"Okay, I'm back." Emily was glad of an excuse to turn her head away and look at Kate.

"I asked you if you want to talk about the immunization idea now or wait till you've wafted Matthew gently down the stream and fed him," Kate said.

"By all means ask him now," Matthew said. "He wouldn't enjoy the trip or the food if he thought it was just to. . . whatever it is."

Though he spoke lightly, there was something in his voice

that told Emily he meant the basic idea behind his words. He wouldn't want anyone to get close to him for any reason other than affection or friendship.

But Kate was off explaining their idea in a rush of enthusiastic words. Matthew turned all his attention to meeting a long logging truck on a sharp curve. Then he looked at Emily in a way that forced her to meet his gaze.

"When were you going to ask me?"

"I don't know," Emily answered honestly. "We just got the idea a day or so ago."

He seemed to be satisfied with her answer. "I think it's a great idea." He spoke faster as his enthusiasm rose. "I've been thinking of having a company picnic before the kids start to school anyway. This would be a perfect time to do it."

"Perfect," Emily said. "We can get the new school kids at the same time. They have to have it."

"But, Emily, even if you give it just for the cost of the serum, there's a lot of families who can't afford it. What if we talk the Public Health Clinic in Clifton into sending someone down and giving it?"

"Oh, that sounds great, Matthew. Even if they can't send someone down, maybe they would let us have the serum to do it," Kate squealed.

"Kate, you sound like a dedicated missionary," Al said affectionately.

Emily felt that twinge of guilt that had become so familiar, and for the first time she wondered why, if God really wanted her to go to Africa, she was getting this heavy and unwanted companion on her shoulder. After all, she wasn't planning anything unethical, and lots of people kept their personal lives private. And, she certainly wasn't leading Matthew to expect anything but friendship.

"Here we are," Matthew interrupted her thoughts, slowing the car to turn off into a lane that led to the River Rat Canoe Rental Camp that nestled on the bank of Cricket Creek. "Al," he threw over his shoulder as he brought the car to a gentle stop, "we now prepare to lean back on a cushion and be wafted down the stream."

"Oh, dear," Al answered, "I forgot to bring my parasol."

On a wave of laughter, they unloaded the lunch and soft drinks from the car and distributed it into two canoes. Then they applied suntan lotion and slipped on safety vests. Though Julie made a face while buckling hers over her skinny body, she didn't argue, as if she knew it would do no good.

Al and Julie had a good-natured argument about where to sit, but finally ended up with Julie plying the front paddle enthusiastically while Kate relaxed elegantly in the center position.

In their canoe, Emily chose to sit in the front and let Matthew guide, but she diligently helped with the rowing. The creek was running slower than it did during the spring rain season and they had to paddle much of the time, but there were deep spots where the canoe danced delightfully as Matthew expertly guided them through.

They came to one enchanting pool nestled in a wide curve that hid the other canoe, which was somewhere behind them. Letting her paddle rest, Emily enjoyed watching in turn the water and the glimpses of busy wildlife on the shore.

"Oh, look, Matthew, there's a fox. He's keeping up with us."

"Where?" Matthew asked, guiding the canoe into shallow water and looking toward the near shore.

"No, no," Emily twisted to see where he was looking. "On the other shore. Look, he's outrunning us." She leaned over and pointed.

Matthew leaned at the same time, looking intently into the trees. Gently and gracefully, the canoe tipped over. It filled with water and scrunched against the gravely bottom while they spilled face forward into the deep pool.

They came up laughing and close together until their safety vests bumped against each other, sending them spinning apart. Instinctively, Matthew reached out and caught Emily by the shoulders to keep her close. He found himself wishing they hadn't been so safety conscious as to wear vests. He would have loved to hold her and feel the water making a soft world of their own around them.

He wanted to kiss her. He watched her blink her eyes against the water that engulfed her when she went face down before her vest righted her. He wanted to kiss the drops of water off.

Did she want that too? Her laughing face wasn't saying yes or no, though she must be reading the longing in his eyes. He leaned toward her and she didn't pull away. Her inviting lips were soft and. . .were they waiting?

Suddenly the canoe carrying Al and Kate darted by. Al yelled and pointed to the foam cooler full of soft drinks that seemed to have found the current and was sailing grandly down the creek.

Grudgingly, Matthew turned loose of Emily's shoulders and waved that he would chase it down. He was positive he saw Kate turn around and throw something squishy at Al.

Working together, they righted the canoe and dipped out the water in it with their big drink cups, which floated near. Then they clambered back in. Matthew took his time working it back into the current. Maybe, just maybe, a chance to find out about that kiss might come again if he let the other canoe get far enough ahead.

Unexpectedly, he heard Emily laughing. Not giggling. She was sitting in the front of the canoe with her head thrown back and guffawing at the top of her lungs.

"You know we were like those, who were they, those people on TV in balloons who kept bouncing off each other every time they tried to get close. . ." She went off into gales of laughter again and Matthew had to join her.

"We're going to have to paddle fast to catch that cooler," she reminded him when they had settled down, driving away any more thoughts of being alone. "Lucky we had the soft drinks instead of the food."

"Sure," Matthew answered, steering them into the middle of the creek. He wondered glumly if she had just very neatly sidestepped any second attempt to kiss her. *At this moment, anyway*, he added to himself.

They came on the others before they located the cooler. "It picked out this nice spot to stop and picnic," Kate called, pointing to the foam container that had become lodged on a gravel bar. "Want to join it?"

"Very much," Emily answered. "I want to take this life vest off and lie in the sun for a day or two and get dry."

"I vote to take a swim while we're wet and let our shorts and shirts lie in the sun and dry out," Matthew put in, stepping out of the canoe and pulling it up on the bar.

"Great. We'll join you," Al agreed. Julie, already in the water, waved to them.

Emily removed the shirt and shorts she was wearing over her swimsuit, and Matthew hung them with his own across a handy bush before he joined them all in the water.

They swam and dived for awhile before they came out and ate chicken sandwiches and potato chips. Matthew searched his shorts pockets for his woodsman's knife and cut a few dry sticks to make a tiny fire for Julie to roast a hot dog, which she chose over chicken sandwiches.

"Like last year," she said, sharing a happy memory with him.

"We all spoil her a little, even Matthew," Kate whispered to Emily with tears in her eyes. "But, oh, it's so good to have my little girl back."

Impulsively, Emily hugged her, feeling tears in her own eyes.

They ate and sat for awhile watching and waving to other boating parties. Then they piled back into the canoes and continued down the creek to the place where they were to be picked up. They were driven back to Matthew's car without another chance for Matthew to test his hope that Emily would have returned his kiss.

eleven

Dear Ryan,

I know how busy you are, but I hope soon you will be able to write me all the details of life in the missionary field.

Short as it was, your letter about immunization made me investigate how many of the local children have been immunized. It turns out, not many until they have to get it to start to school. So we're having a big day at the clinic. We found out that even if we waive the fee for giving the shots, the cost is still higher than some of the local people can pay.

The owner of the furniture factory here and I went to the Public Health Department at Clifton and got them to agree to give us serum and so we can hold an immunization clinic here. It's next Wednesday. The workers at the lumber company and the furniture factory (that's just about everybody around these parts) are having a picnic then at the factory, which is just next door to the clinic, so we hope to get at least all those children. Kate and I will give them a shot and send

*them back to the picnic for ice cream. Keep
your fingers crossed.*

> *Oh, we're also going to get as many
women as we can to come over for
mammograms. Do you do those there?
Forgive me if I ask foolish questions, but I
have such a skimpy idea of your work. Later,
maybe you'll have time to fill me in.*

*Love,
Emily*

Emily leaned back at her desk in the front room of her house, feeling an odd sense of relief at getting the letter to Ryan finished. *Why don't I say Matthew's name to him?* she asked herself. *Can it be for the same reason he doesn't write the name of the nurse who keeps everybody able to do their work? Are we drifting apart?*

She reminded herself that this possibility was her reason for refusing to become engaged to Ryan. Even if she went to the mission field, she had to accept the fact that it might not be as Ryan's wife.

Even if? Was she wavering? But surely she wouldn't have had the intense desire to go if it wasn't God's will. Was she so lacking in purpose that she let just anyone or anything change her plans?

Silently, she relaxed herself with folded hands and prayed that God would show her what His plans for her were. "And, God" she added, "help us make tomorrow a success and a good day for this community. And sunshine would be nice for the picnic."

She smiled as she realized that the prayer itself made her want to make a last minute inspection at the clinic to be sure everything was ready. Slipping sandals over her bare feet and a small flashlight in the back pocket of her jeans, she went out to the sidewalk without bothering to get her car out. The short walk would do her good.

She had been called back to the clinic too many times in the middle of the night to let its lonely silence bother her. Using her key at the back door, she went in through the tiny kitchen. She didn't have to check for the serum. She knew that Kate and Cammie had taken all the food out of the small refrigerator and cleaned it thoroughly so they could store the serum there. She went on through to the front, where a low light burned all night.

She flicked on the upper light and stood at the desk. Knowing that she didn't dare touch Cammie's efficiently planned stacks of papers or her files, she wondered why she was here. She turned off the light and went back to the exam rooms.

Boxes of extra disposable syringes and needles were lined up on convenient shelves. Kate had everything ready here. They planned for Cammie to bring the children back to them after she had done the proper paper work. Kate would work in one exam room while Emily worked in the other.

There was nothing more to be done. Emily turned out the lights. She was preparing to leave when she heard the front buzzer sound. Flicking on the overhead light as she went through the waiting room, she opened the door, expecting someone in distress.

Matthew stood there. He broke into a relieved grin when

he saw her. "Well, I'm glad it's you. I saw the lights moving around and didn't see your car or Kate's, so I thought I'd better see if someone's breaking in. It's a great relief not to have to be a hero and save the serum." He stepped in and closed the door.

Emily laughed. "I decided the walk over would be good for me. I'm too excited about tomorrow to settle down. What are you doing here so late?"

Even as she asked, she found herself retreating behind Cammie's desk, uncomfortably aware that her actions showed a ridiculous nervousness at being alone with Matthew.

"Well, what are you doing here so late?" he responded. "Can I help you with anything?" He moved to the counter across from her and leaned on it. "Anything that a non-medical person can do?"

"I asked you first. And Kate and Cammie seem to have everything set up. I don't dare touch anything, myself."

"O.K. I came over to the factory to be sure everything is ready for the picnic tomorrow. I want this to be a real family event and for everyone to have fun at my party even if they won't at yours."

Emily grinned. "I prayed for sunshine."

"What a coincidence. So did I." They laughed together.

Then Matthew looked at her seriously. Even with the desk and counter between them, Emily had the impression that he was towering over her.

Matthew looked across the counter at Emily. *She's like a lovely tropical fish*, he thought, *always just slipping past me, almost but not quite close enough to touch. Does she have any idea how much I want to get past that. . .whatever barrier it is that she's putting up against me? Sometime I have to make her know.*

"Why are you hiding from me, Emily?"

"Why, Matthew, I'm not hiding. I'm standing here in plain sight. I'm just. . .checking that all the papers are here." She didn't look up.

"You just said Kate and Cammie have everything ready and you don't dare touch anything."

She smiled, nervously. "I did say that, didn't I? But I didn't mean that I couldn't check on them."

All right, beautiful fish, I'll let you slip by this time, he thought, *but some day. . .some day, I'll make you stop and deal with me. And some day, some future day, maybe we'll will be close enough I can even tell you I called you a fish.*

Out loud he said, "Then let's go over to the Blue Bird for some of your mom's great pie."

With a sigh of relief that he thought she might be unaware of, she agreed.

The atmosphere at the Blue Bird was far from relaxed. Everybody who worked there or who could be coaxed into service scurried about preparing the picnic goodies that Al was catering.

"Your mom's back in the kitchen," Al said, as he slapped big wedges of chocolate cream pie and coffee on their table. "She's got Ben doing dirty dish duty. I just sent Kate home, though, so she'll be sharp tomorrow. You'd better do the same, Doc."

"I'll see that she does as soon as we finish appreciating

your superb service," Matthew called lightly to Al's departing back. Al gave him a quick wave of his hand without turning around.

When they had finished their pie and coffee, they wandered back to the kitchen and found a scene of what looked like total confusion. Bread and sandwich makings were piled everywhere. Everyone seemed to be moving in crosscurrents but, after watching awhile, they could see that Caroline was directing each person to a specific task.

"Unless you came to peel potatoes, go away," Caroline called pleasantly. "You're using up the oxygen."

Laughing, Matthew and Emily decided to take the best of her options and backed out. But Emily was almost sure that her mother took a second from her work to look at them with a pleased grin. She determined to remind Caroline of Ryan some time soon.

"I'll go get my car and drive you home," Matthew said when they stood on the sidewalk in front of the cafe.

"I'd rather walk," Emily replied, remembering her mother's expression. "But thanks, anyway."

"Fine." Matthew ignored her dismissal. "We'll walk. It would be a shame not to savor this moonlight. Must be full."

"It was full last night," Emily answered absently. "Even these ugly little buildings look good in moonlight." She forced herself to wonder what Africa looked like in moonlight and who Ryan might share it with.

"Do you see Sawtown as ugly?" Matthew sounded surprised.

"Well, you have to admit, it looks a great deal like its

name."

"Yes, I guess it does," he answered without trying to defend the town further.

Emily wished he would argue more. She couldn't think of any way to break their silence and he was walking much too close to her. Her disloyal mind seemed to be letting her fall into the relaxed, agreeable mood that he was obviously enjoying.

He reached out and took her hand and, somehow, there didn't seem to be a reason to pull away.

When they reached her house, he guided her around it to the patio in the back. "Let's just sit here for a while and drink it in," he said softly, drawing her to a chair and taking one for himself that was close enough he didn't have to let her hand go.

Emily might have argued, but at that moment she caught sight of a shadow just beyond the dry stream at the edge of the trees.

"Sssh," she whispered. "There he is."

"There who is?"

"The dog. It's a huge, big brown and white that looks like a wolf, sort of. He comes there and I've been putting out food that he eats sometime when I'm not around. But he won't come closer."

"Oh. Boone."

"Boone?"

"Daniel Boone. He's an adventurer. Likes to be alone. He comes to the mill, too. Sometimes when the men are cutting he sits down and watches them. Everybody tries to take him home, but he's an independent cuss. Wants to be his own dog."

Emily drew away and pulled her hand from his. "Then I won't keep hoping he'll come away from the cutting down of trees and move in with me," she said coolly. She stood up. "I really need to go in now. I have to be alert tomorrow."

"Good night, Emily. Sleep well." Matthew stood and turned away, then waited to see that she got in without any problem. What had happened to change her? They had seemed to be so close, so much in the same dreamy mood. Was she playing some kind of childish game with him? But everything he had seen of Dr. Emily Richards told him she wasn't a silly coquette who got a sick pleasure out of flirting and shying away like someone's idea of an old-fashioned southern belle.

With a sudden determination, he turned back and walked toward her. She could wait until she was ready to tell him why she always slipped away from him, but now he was going to kiss her.

He put his hands on her shoulders as she fumbled with her key at the door and gently turned her around to face him. He looked into her questioning eyes for a minute then, without moving his hands from her shoulders or pulling her closer to him, he leaned forward and put his mouth on hers. Her lips were soft and supple under his, neither responding nor repelling him.

He held them with his own for a long, tender moment before he felt a flutter of response. Then there was no doubt that she was kissing him back, as the moon turned its light off for everyone but them.

He lifted his head and caught her face in both hands, looking deeply into her eyes and seeing no coolness there.

"There," he said, with satisfaction. "There." Without trying to explain what the words meant to him, he took her key, opened her door and held it for her.

"Good night," he said again. He was pretty sure she didn't answer him.

Emily walked into her kitchen and bumped into the table before she thought of turning on the light. Had she been subconsciously wondering what it would be like to be kissed by Matthew since the canoe trip when it had been so close? Well, it was. . .not like being kissed by Ryan which, she had to admit to herself, had never caused her to bump into tables.

It was. . .it was time to go to bed in order to be alert in the morning just as she had sensibly told Matthew earlier. Much earlier. Eons earlier. Before the kiss.

Emily went to bed and, if she didn't sleep well, each time she woke it was with undefined happy thoughts.

Her thoughts in the morning were more down-to-earth. Matthew and everybody else must be told about Ryan and, somehow, without disturbing the town's confidence until she could recruit Joyce or another doctor for them, that there was a limit on her time here. She didn't want to feel inside herself that she was misleading anyone, even though she would fulfill her own commitment to the community.

She wished she didn't feel such a lilt every time the evening before passed through her mind.

Even after she went in to the clinic, she continued to let the problem run through her mind. However, a short time with the enthusiasm of Kate and Cammie brought her attention back to the purpose of the day, and she determined to put both Matthew and Ryan out of her mind for this day.

Matthew and his crew had organized games for the children in the morning while the women came to the clinic for mammograms.

Jane Smith, the mammogram technician, arrived shortly after Emily did, and women started drifting in soon afterwards. By mid-morning the waiting room was full of women, who carried the picnic atmosphere into the clinic, and the room resounded with laughter and talk.

"How many?" Emily asked Cammie when the last one had gone back to the tables spread under trees in the factory grounds.

"Would you accept twenty as a pretty good start?" Cammie asked, grinning.

Emily smiled back and went to thank Jane, who was preparing to carry her films back to Clifton to be read by a radiologist. She declined to go over for the picnic.

Kate and Emily and Cammie hurriedly ate picnic food that Al brought over. Then they prepared for a hoped-for influx of children.

The children weren't as bright and cheerful as their mothers had been but Emily, as she administered serum and lollipops, knew that they would soon forget the short ouch. They were to go back to the air-conditioned lunchroom in the factory for ice cream and a fun program.

After they were through with the immunizations, the three women went over to the lunchroom in the factory, where the children had been handed ice cream as they came back from the clinic. They were now seated with their parents for the entertainment that had been worked up by the church members.

Reverend Adams was a middling magician, but children always responded to his personality. Two of the church-women had worked up an almost thrilling puppet show and the crowd (except possibly some of the children) was now so pleased with the events of the day that they applauded enthusiastically, even when one of them forgot her part.

Everyone knew Angeline Adams was the clown. She was always available to do her Christian Clown act for any event in the community. The short, plump wife of Reverend Adams was so full of childlike joy in living that though they had seen her many times before, people of all ages responded happily to her whether she was in clown costume or the more formal clothes she normally wore.

When the event began to break up and people left, calling out good-byes and teasing each other about the amount of food consumed, even the child who had cried hardest at being "shot" went home happy.

twelve

Dear Emily,

The need here is enormous. Sometimes it seems like everybody in Africa is going from one place to another in search of safety or food or some kind of health care. It's impossible for us to have enough medical people to take care of them.

I understand that you want to know more details and eventually I know I will be able to write them to you but now, I guess you could say, I'm still in a kind of cultural shock. The nurse I mentioned before said she had the same thing when she first came here. She said you never get used to what you see, but eventually you learn to cope with it in some kind of way so you at least sleep at night. I'm not sure I would have managed to cope the little bit I have if she hadn't been here to help me.

I'm sorry my letters aren't better, Emily. I'm still looking forward to you joining me. Two years is a long time.

Love,
Ryan

Emily took a long drink of her iced cappuccino, then put

the glass down in displeasure.

Here I sit in my comfortable patio, she thought, *watching what I've decided to call my dog come across the ravine to get the food I've put out for him. I'm drinking my favorite drink, after fixing myself a good meal, and I know my comfortable bed is inside waiting for me whenever I choose to go in. While in this world there are people who have to go from place to place looking for the very basics of life. And people like Ryan and this nurse he writes about live in conditions I can't even imagine while they try to give some relief to the poorest of the poor.*

Surely this letter is a signal to me that I must start letting those people closest to me know that I will be leaving when Joyce can come. And I need to start asking her to make the decision. Maybe she's ready to visit me here, like we talked about before I left St. Louis. I'll write her tonight.

And after she visits I'll remind Mom that I was interested in the missionary field and I'll tell Kate. And I'll tell Matthew. I owe him that much. She found herself remembering his kiss. *Unless, maybe he just likes doctors and will fall for Joyce. I'll do what everyone around me is doing. I'll play matchmaker. I'll write her now.*

❧

The answer came by return mail. Emily understood the underlying stress it showed, even though Joyce didn't express it.

> *Dear Emily,*
> *Your letter came at just the right time. I feel like I need to get away for a while and Mom and Dad are full up with visiting*

*people who will be doing all the city things I
don't want to do now. Will Friday, August 25,
be a good time? Just for the weekend.*

Love,

Joyce

Emily called Joyce immediately and they made plans. "I can't tell you how much I'm looking forward to having you here and showing you what attractions Sawtown has," she teased.

"Emily, you sound like you've got something interesting up your sleeve. I'll be happy just to sit on that back patio you tell me about and watch your dog. I'm getting away from a lot of social stuff."

"Don't worry. Society here isn't what you'd call high, but it's friendly. We'll sit on the patio Friday, but I want to show you a little of Arkansas's charms Saturday."

As she put the phone down, Emily wondered what she could do to make Joyce want to come to Sawtown. Cricket Creek was almost too low for canoeing in the August heat.

She found Kate the next morning at her desk, reading a stack of papers.

"Kate, I need help."

"I'll be there in just a minute, Doctor. Is it an emergency? I didn't hear anyone come in."

"No" Emily asked. "It's not doctor help. It's Emily help."

Kate looked up, questions in her eyes. A happy smile flashed across her face.

Emily laughed. "Oh, Kate, it isn't help with my personal life, either. I have a friend from St. Louis coming down for the week-end. She wants to get away from city life."

"Well, that should be easy," Kate said dryly.

"But what can I do to show her what a great place Arkansas is? Can you and Al help? I'm meeting her at the Little Rock Airport Friday and taking her back after church Sunday so we really only have Saturday."

"Mmm," Kate leaned back. "Let me see if I can think of a handsome hunk to go with us. Besides Matthew, I mean."

"Oh, we don't need another man, Emily. I'm not trying to get her married this weekend. We can be a fivesome. If Matthew will be available."

"Oh, I think he will be. He seems to have become one of the most available men I know recently."

Emily decided to ignore that. "O.K. Have any ideas about what we should do? There are so many things in Arkansas to show her, but she really wants to get away from people."

"We'll think of something good." Kate patted the papers on her desk and her expression became serious as she changed the subject. "These are reports on the mammograms. Two women have lumps. Angeline Adams is one. And Chloe Logan, who works as a finisher in the furniture factory."

Immediately Emily forgot Joyce's coming visit and turned her mind to those two women. "I'll go over and tell Angeline and Ethan. Can you catch Mrs. Logan at the factory now before patients come in? Then we'll make arrangements for them to see Dr. Anderson in Clifton. He'll want to do biopsies."

Driving over to the Adams' small house, just off Main Street, Emily prayed for help in telling Angeline. She felt that she had received it when Angeline met her at the door.

"Emily. If you're here this early on an office day, there must be a problem. Is it mine or one of our church people's?"

Emily could only answer such a brave attitude with honesty. "Yours, Angeline," she said quietly.

"Well, come on in." Angeline's expression sobered but she didn't try to flinch away. "Ethan is right in the kitchen."

Emily followed her through the pleasant living room to the kitchen, which was the biggest room in the house. Reverend Adams was sitting at the old round table in the middle of the room, drinking coffee. He motioned for Emily to join him. "Or do I need to go with you right away?" he asked.

"No." Emily sat and accepted a cup of coffee from Angeline.

Angeline went around the table and sat beside her husband. "It's about time the mammogram reports came back. Is it about that?"

"Yes. There's a shadow in your left breast, Angeline. You know this doesn't necessarily mean that it's malignant, but we need to set you up an appointment with a surgeon in Clifton. I recommend Dr. Anderson, who is particularly interested in problems of the breast."

Reverend Adams' face stiffened as he clutched Angeline's hand, but her plump face remained serene. "Of course, Emily. Whenever he can see me. And, Ethan, don't you dare go mentally picking out a place to bury me. We'll wait to see what the Lord wills but, unless He objects, I plan to live a long time yet."

Ethan managed a laugh. After talking a bit, Emily left. She was sure that, with her attitude, even if the lump turned out to be malignant, Angeline would live a long time yet.

When she got back to the clinic, she found Kate almost in tears. "Mrs. Logan is frantic. She's already decided she's dying, in spite of my attempts to reassure her. She's almost angry with us for making her know she has a lump and with me for coming over to tell her. I promised to make her an appointment for tomorrow. She can't handle waiting very long."

"I'm sure Dr. Anderson will understand. His nurse has been told to juggle appointments to get people like her in quickly. Angeline is totally calm, but get her in as soon as possible too."

"I'll call right away. Oh, and I talked to Matthew before I found Mrs. Logan. He suggests that we take your friend to the Crater of Diamonds. That's about as far from city life as you can get. Then maybe rent a boat and go out on one of the lakes."

"I'd almost forgotten about Joyce. But she'll get a kick out of that. I can still remember how thrilled I was as a kid to think that I was a real diamond miner. Of course I always expected to find the world's biggest diamond."

"Maybe this time you will, in a way."

Once again, Emily decided to ignore any symbolism in Kate's remark.

❧

"Why didn't you tell me Arkansas is so beautiful?" Joyce asked.

"I thought I did. But you know, you just have to be there."

They were traveling out from Little Rock in that magic moment just before the sun started sliding behind the mountains. Emily stole a glance away from her driving to look at Joyce.

"You don't look like someone suffering from stress. You look marvelous, Joyce. And you still have that darkly beautiful, sophisticated model look."

Joyce made a throw it away gesture. "There's no temptation to put on any extra pounds in the quote, 'hospital milieu,' unquote. What about the stress of being the only doctor in a thousand miles of wilderness?"

Emily laughed. "Dr. Anderson in Clifton takes calls for me every blue moon. He'll do it tomorrow while we show you that wilderness. Believe it or not, we're going to take you diamond mining."

"Diamond mining? Emily, do you have some weird plot in mind? Like a love at first sight for me?"

"Joyce, I am solemnly, truthfully telling you that you will go diamond hunting for real diamonds in a real diamond mine. The only one in the U.S. I think."

Emily could feel Joyce's dark eyes on her even in the fading light. "Why do I feel a smattering of evasion in that answer? But, I'll keep my suspicions to myself until I see this way of looking for a diamond. It's certainly not the method my mom keeps planning for me."

"Good. Now, next time you come, I'll take you to the hospital in Clifton, but this time I just want to show you the clinic and have a fun day tomorrow."

"What about this man who's moving in on Ryan in your life?"

"Joyce, I've never said Matt—any man is moving in. In fact, I thought you might be interested in meeting Matthew Barnes, like you're going to do tomorrow."

Joyce laughed. "I'm very sharp at reading between the lines, Dr. Emily Richards. Don't expect me to be the wall you want to put up. But tell me, is he really as handsome as you say he is?"

"I didn't say he was. . .oh, you're just teasing."

Joyce laughed and Emily changed the subject by asking about what had happened since she left St. Louis. It took Joyce the rest of the trip to bring her up-to-date, and after showing her the clinic and giving her a cup of herbal tea in her kitchen, Emily insisted that Joyce should go to bed and get a good night's sleep.

"So you can be bright-eyed and beautiful tomorrow," she said.

"Emily, how many times must I tell you I won't take Matthew over for you? You're going to have to make your own decision about those two men."

"I didn't—"

"Just reading between the lines again." With a flip of her hand, Joyce disappeared into the guest room.

Emily sat there for a long time, staring into her empty tea cup. Was she really that transparent? She was going to have to tell everyone about her plans with Ryan. Starting with Matthew. Just as soon as Joyce left.

Trying to put it all out of her mind for now, she busied herself searching her closet for floppy hats for herself and Joyce to wear against the intense sun they would be experiencing in the search for diamonds. Much later, she felt calm enough to go to sleep.

Emily noticed with disappointment that Kate and Al already had Matthew in their large, late model car when they came to pick her and Joyce up. She had hoped to maneuver Joyce into sitting in front in Matthew's car.

Instead, after general introductions, the three of them settled into the back seat with Matthew in the center. At least, she thought ruefully, the seat was wide enough that they had ample room. She carefully snuggled against the side of the car while they exchanged small talk as they rode through the green hills to Crater of Diamonds State Park.

"Is everybody thoroughly covered with sunscreen?" Kate

asked as they piled out of the car in the parking lot of the park. "That sun is murder out there in August."

"Every spare inch, though I really didn't expect to get sunburned in a diamond mine. I thought we'd be going into the depths of the earth." Joyce bent to add a glob of lotion to her already well-tanned legs, looking lovely in wide-legged shorts. Emily, who hadn't found much time for swimming, was wearing light slacks and shirt, as was Kate.

A friendly attendant in the park building gave them each a trowel and a wire-bottomed container to sift out the dirt.

"Only diamonds don't go through the holes," Matthew explained seriously as they went into the fenced area already sparsely filled with hunters.

"You know," Joyce set her feet stubbornly in the soft earth, looking out at the dry expanse before them. "I'm not such a city slicker that I don't recognize a snipe hunt when I see one. You all Arkansans are leading me into a funny. This is just a plowed field. I bet the man just pulled his corn up yesterday."

The friendly laughter and cajoling that followed put them all into a light-hearted mood as each of the others simultaneously tried to convince Joyce either that it was or wasn't a hoax. Finally Matthew took her by the hand and led her into the field as Emily heard him explaining truthfully that it was the cone of an ancient and extinct volcano and that there really were diamonds to be found there.

He stayed with her all during the time they dug, and Emily could hear them chattering as enthusiastically as children while they sifted dirt, their heads close together.

"Emily, you're not supposed to try to dig clear to the bottom of the volcano, you know. Or are you getting ready to bury a body?"

"Burying a body, I'd guess, from the vicious way she's slinging that dirt."

Emily looked up in surprise to see Al and Kate standing over her, then down at the hole she had dug without thinking about it. Her container was piled high with dirt, and she caught herself in the process of adding another trowel full to it.

Telling herself that her violent digging had nothing to do with the apparent success of her plan to throw Matthew and Joyce together, Emily pretended not to notice that Al and Kate seemed to be trying to stifle laughter.

Matthew and Joyce joined them then. "We've decided that the nicest thing we can find now is a big, big swimming pool. Like a lake," Matthew said. Then, looking at Emily's sifter, "Just as soon as we help Emily search her hoard."

Laughing again, they all took some of the dirt from Emily's container. Matthew found a garnet and solemnly presented it to Joyce, "to remember us by."

"I'll keep it always. Or at least almost," Joyce assured him.

They drove a short distance to a breathtakingly lovely little lake. In a glass-fronted restaurant overlooking the lake, they dug ravenously into huge hamburgers and french fries. Then, while the men rented a boat, the women retired to a dressing room to change to swim suits.

Matthew took them at a slow pace about the lake for an hour or so before he stopped the motor and dropped the anchor near a gently wooded shore so they could swim and float. Matthew seemed to divide his attention equally between Joyce and Emily.

Emily wondered if he was being careful not to make her feel as if he was too interested in Joyce, then chided herself for being childish.

At mid-afternoon, they headed in to the dock. On the trip back to Sawtown, Joyce stretched her lovely long legs and napped, her head drifting over against Matthew's shoulder. The others in the car settled into a quiet relaxed atmosphere that lasted until they arrived at Emily's house. Emily was careful not to catch Matthew's eye and tried not to think of how successful her half-formed plan to get Matthew and Joyce to like each other seemed to be.

"This was the most out-of-this-world day I've spent recently. Well, rather more than recently," Joyce said, as they emerged from the car, clutching their wet bathing suits and floppy hats. "No one will believe me when I tell them I actually went mining. Thanks for giving me something to prove it." She showed Matthew that she still had the stone.

"Thank Emily," Matthew said, grinning. "She was the one who dug it out of the depths."

"Only doing my duty as a good hostess." Emily hoped she sounded as frivolous as Matthew and wondered if he suspected (wrongly, she insisted to herself) that his attentions to Joyce might have caused the wild digging.

He only smiled and assured them both that he would pick them up later to go out to Caroline's.

Caroline and Ben had invited them all to a barbecue at their house, but Al and Kate had to beg off because they had promised Julie to help her with a Sunday school project. Matthew drove Joyce and Emily out.

Emily insisted on sitting in the back seat, "so Joyce can see better." Joyce gave a discreetly lowered snort, which Emily thought Matthew pretended not to hear. Nevertheless, he dutifully pointed out the different trees that lined the narrow lane down to the house. Joyce, in her turn, dutifully pretended to be interested.

They found Caroline in the kitchen. After Emily had introduced Joyce, Caroline gave them tall glasses of spiced tea and shooed them out of the kitchen to help Ben, who was smoking a small turkey. They found him relaxing with a glass of tea far enough away from the smoker to keep cool.

"By all means, sit right down and help me keep this turkey from flying away," Ben said, after he had taken Joyce's hand deep into his big one and commented on the fact that doctors were getting more beautiful every day. They laughed and took seats about the terrace.

"Ben, is the turkey about ready?" Caroline called from the kitchen.

"Hon, he's just been waiting for you," Ben called back.

"Well, bring him in and let's cut him up in here. Everything else is ready, too."

Ben expertly slid the beautifully browned turkey from the grill to a platter and took it in, refusing their assistance. "Just stay out here and watch the sun go away," he said. "Caroline and I will be out in two shakes with the food."

They sat quietly, as he suggested, falling into a dreamy mood as shadows settled over the forest, while somewhere back in the trees, a crow cawed out his lonesome cry. Happily tired from the sun and water they had enjoyed, they let the comfortable silence of friends settle over them.

"Emily," Joyce spoke dreamily, as if almost napping again, "if I take your practice over here when you go to Ryan in Africa, I'm going to insist that your mom let me come out here whenever I need to recharge my batter—"

She stopped abruptly, sensing the sudden change of mood among them. Emily felt her muscles tense in painful knots. This was the worst possible way for Matthew to find out that she didn't plan to stay in Sawtown past her committed time. Why, oh, why hadn't she told him before?

She forced herself to lift her face and look into the blazing anger in his eyes.

Caroline and Ben came out then, bringing food. They seemed surprised at the change in atmosphere and spent the rest of the frustrating evening trying to cope with something they couldn't understand. Though Emily and Joyce attempted to help dispel the mood, Matthew remained grimly quiet.

He was polite to Joyce on the way home, but Emily knew he was waiting until they were alone to discuss her plans with her.

"Emily, I'm sorry," Joyce said, as soon as they were alone in Emily's living room. "I didn't realize that you hadn't told Matthew."

"It wasn't your fault, Joyce. I should have told him. I've been planning to and just putting it off. At first I didn't think it was any of his business. My last excuse was that I would tell him after you'd visited."

"You mean after I'd visited and Matthew and I had fallen in love at first sight and removed the whole problem of Matthew and Ryan? It's not going to happen, Emily. Matthew is a fascinating man and maybe over time, I might fall for him, but he couldn't even see me for looking at your face. You're just going to have to make some decisions, Emily. Matthew is too great a person to be kept hoping as he so obviously is. . .was."

Emily caught Joyce's hand. "Joyce, it's true. I was. I hate to admit it but, subconsciously, at least, I was hoping to use you to settle my problem with Matthew. Please forgive me."

"It would have been a great way to be used if it had worked, Emily. Of course I forgive you. May none of my friends try to use me in anything worse than that. But I think you're still evading the real issue. Do you stay or do you go? Do you really love Ryan or the idea of Africa? Is that current that jumps between you and Matthew something most people call love? I'm not as great in the praying department as you, but I think it's about that time."

"You're right, it is," Emily said, thoughtfully. "I do need help."

But it was hard to find the right words, after she and Joyce had finally decided to give up and go to bed. Every time she tried to couch her needs in prayer, Ryan's and Matthew's faces interfered with her thoughts and Matthew's was always angry.

"God," she finally prayed, "I know it isn't Matthew or Ryan but what You want me to do with my life and the healing arts I've been taught. Please guide me and forgive any wrong I may have done by not being totally honest with those closest to me."

With these words, she finally slept.

thirteen

"Emily, we need to talk."

Emily had hardly arrived home from driving Joyce to the airport when her doorbell rang. As she expected, Matthew stood there. Silently, she turned and walked into her living room. If he wanted to consider that an invitation to follow her, he could.

He did. She sank into a corner of the couch, and he sat in an arm chair directly across from her. The silly thought ran through her mind that she should rearrange the furniture. She felt like she was literally being pinned against the back of the couch.

"Are you an ex-wrestler, by any chance?"

The question seemed to throw him off key. "I suppose there must be a reason you asked that."

Emily decided not to explain. "Not a very good one," she admitted.

Matthew continued to stare at her. "Do you want to talk first, or do I have to pry the rest of it out of you? And don't ask me what I'm talking about."

"I won't." Emily felt her defiance slipping away. "I meant to tell you, Matthew."

Matthew waited silently, trying not to let her obvious distress deter him. He hadn't slept at all and his emotions had run up and down like chills and fever, but sometime in

145

the night he knew exactly how he felt about Emily. What he wanted now was for her to tell him that Joyce was making a bad joke, and everything in him knew that she wasn't going to do that.

"I had decided after that night—"

"When I kissed you."

She nodded. "Up until then I could tell myself that it wasn't any of your business but when—"

"You kissed me back. You liked the kiss."

Again she nodded, without trying to look away from his eyes. "Then I decided I'd tell you after Joyce left so you wouldn't be mad while she was here."

"So you let her tell me, instead."

"I didn't mean. . .she didn't mean. . .she just didn't think."

He pushed back the temptation to walk over to her, pull her to her feet, and remind her why she had liked the first kiss. But if what Joyce had said meant what it seemed to, he had scruples about kissing someone who was planning to marry another man. Especially someone who had returned his kiss the first time without telling him about the other man.

"Make me understand, Emily. Let's start out with basics. First of all, who is this man in Africa?"

"He's a doctor I worked with in St. Louis."

"And?"

"And he finished his residency about the same time I did. We worked together a lot. We felt the same about our profession. We respected each other. We dated the last year."

"And?"

"His church put him through medical school with the

understanding that he would go into missionary work."

"And?"

"Will you please stop saying that?"

"Do you want to tell me all of it, and I do mean all, without being pressed? When are you planning to go back on your commitment to Sawtown?"

She jerked herself upright. "Matthew, I'm not ever going back on my commitment. I came down here with every intention of being ethical about that, and I still do. You can question my honesty in not telling you about Ryan and Africa, but you can't question my ethics. I'll stay here for the two years I promised. And I plan to find a replacement if I leave. Probably Joyce. Don't you think she was favorably impressed with Arkansas? You did everything you could to make her like us."

Emily caught her breath, wishing with all her heart that she could take that last remark back.

"I was only trying to please you by helping your guest enjoy herself. If I had known all your ulterior motives, I might have tried harder. Was that what you wanted? To use me to help her decide to come here so you could go to another man in another place?"

Emily felt her body tense till she was aware of backbone pressing against the couch. "Oh, Matthew, I'd never use you." Then she slumped, accepting the truth. She forced herself to look into the dark intensity of his eyes. "I wasn't thinking of it as using you," she admitted slowly, "but I did have an idea in mind that you and Joyce might. . .that if I leave. . ."

"If you leave or when you leave? Which is it?"

"I'm not sure. I was sure when I came here, at least I think I was, but I'm not sure now." Again she didn't flinch from meeting his eyes.

He pressed relentlessly on with his questions. "And what about this man who is willing to wait for you for two years? Are you engaged?"

"Not really. I wouldn't become engaged to him until I was free to go to Africa." She hesitated. This angry man in front of her might not believe what she wanted to say, but somewhere inside him was the Matthew she had come to know as thoughtful and generous.

"Matthew, I really believed when I finished my training that God wanted me to be a medical missionary. Even now, when I get a letter telling me about conditions there, I feel like I'm taking the easy way here. But when something happens like us doing mammograms and maybe saving lives, I feel needed here. I'm torn. And He doesn't seem to be giving me any answer."

Matthew knew that if he stayed there a minute longer, he'd pull her into his arms and cradle her until she knew where she wanted to stay. But the decision had to be hers. He wasn't going to kiss her again until she had put the other man out of her life. And somewhere in the back of his mind he reluctantly accepted that she might later suffer from guilt if she let him swerve her from a course she deeply believed God wanted her to follow. No, if she came to him, she had to come free from any doubts. Free from either love or conscience pushing her to hesitate to stay in Sawtown.

"Emily, I know that the official commitment was for two years, but Sawtown floated that bond and built that clinic because they believed that the doctor who grew up here and knew its needs would come back to stay. It's between you and God where you think you should serve Him, but this other thing is between you and me. I love you. I want you to know that. I want to marry you. I'll even take my forestry experience to the mission field with you if that is what you decide you should do. But I won't be back until you tell me that Ryan is out of your life."

He turned and went out. The door closed softly behind him, but Emily heard the finality in it. She wasn't sure how long she sat there before she could move even to go to bed.

Her years in residency had taught her to sleep whenever she had an opportunity, so she went to the office on Monday feeling fairly rested but miserably unhappy.

Her spirits rose when Dr. Anderson called from Clifton about noon to tell her that the preliminary report on Mrs. Logan's biopsy was benign. He had taken her in on an emergency basis because of her intense despair at having the lump discovered.

"You suddenly look shiny all over your face." Kate stopped by the open door of Emily's office as she put down the phone. "It must have been good news." Her grin told Emily she was thinking, *It must have been Matthew.*

"It was great news. Mrs. Logan's biopsy is finished and the lump isn't malignant. Now let's hope Angeline's will be benign, too. When have we set her up for a biopsy?"

"She's to see Dr. Anderson tomorrow. But she says she can't have the biopsy until after Helen Embrey's wedding, because Helen expects her to play her favorite songs. That will make it about Friday."

Emily nodded. "I would expect her to put everybody else's needs ahead of her own. Just let's be sure she doesn't find someone who needs her after that. Oh," she swiveled her chair around so she wasn't looking directly at Kate, "we promised to let the people at the factory know about Mrs. Logan. Will you call Matthew, please, and tell him?"

"I have to get both exam rooms set up and several charts ready for you to sign. Maybe you could call him." Emily could hear a mischievous lilt in Kate's voice.

"Kate," she said without turning or smiling, "please take time to call Matthew."

"Of course," Kate said in her best nurse to doctor voice. But it held a note of surprise and perhaps a hint of hurt feelings. Emily immediately felt regret for letting her own pain lash out at such a good friend. She swiveled her chair back to apologize, but Kate was gone.

If Kate's feelings were hurt she didn't show it as they worked together for the rest of the day. At lunch she told Emily that Matthew was out somewhere in the forest with the sawyers, but that she had given the message to his factory foreman. Though Emily knew she must be wondering why she had suddenly been so adamant about refusing to talk to Matthew, and had perhaps put that together with Matthew's retreat to the forest, Kate didn't pry.

When the clinic closed, Emily didn't go home. She knew that Caroline and Ben would be glad to share their meal with her and she went directly to the house by the forest.

She was relieved to find that Caroline was alone, eating a salad on the patio. "Don't move," Emily said. "I'll go in and make myself one exactly like that—and do I still have instant cappuccino here? Iced would be nice."

"I think so, Emily. In the second shelf on the right."

When she brought out her salad and a glass of iced cappuccino, she sat across the table from Caroline in what would normally have been a comfortable silence.

Today, Caroline seemed to sense her distress. "Did you have a bad day at the office, hon?"

"Fairly slow." Emily took a carefully casual sip of her coffee without meeting Caroline's eyes.

"Nothing bad happened at the house, I hope. No dripping faucets, stopped up toilets?"

Emily gave up and laughed. "Mom, you sound like you used to when I was in high school and you intuited that I was upset. And you know what? You were usually right."

"So am I right now? And do you want to talk about it?"

Emily felt her smile twisting into a frown. She studied the trees, silent now in the August heat.

"Mom, you know I've told you about Ryan and that he's in Africa."

Caroline sighed. "And hinted that you might want to join him sometime. But I've hoped. . .maybe that's why I've pushed you and Matthew a little bit—but then I would have anyway because he's such great son-in-law material. But that didn't work, did it?"

Emily lifted her glass up and down, watching the series of wet circles appear on the table. "It may have, Mom." She wiped the circles dry with her napkin. "He kissed me."

"No." Caroline widened her mouth in exaggeration. "I'll get out my gun."

"All right, funny woman. But I hadn't planned to kiss anyone but Ryan from now on. And I certainly hadn't planned to. . .I never reacted to Ryan's kiss like I did

Matthew's."

Caroline's expression was serious as she placed her hand over Emily's cold one. "I don't really want to push you in any direction, sweetheart, because it's your life and you have to make peace with yourself and God about what you do with it, not with me. But you know I hope you'll stay in Sawtown."

"Mom, I've prayed but I don't think God is listening. Maybe He doesn't care what I do with my life."

"He's listening, honey, and He cares. But He isn't going to force you. Sometimes He's willing to wait on you and you have to be willing to wait on Him."

"Joyce let it slip to Matthew that I planned to go to Ryan in Africa. He thinks I'm not being fair with Sawtown even if I stay two years. Do you?"

"You're asking me an honest question. I have to give you an honest answer. Sawtown has acted as it has, expecting you to stay. You aren't obligated beyond two years, but there will be disappointment."

"But if Joyce comes?"

"Will someone who thinks now that she wants to get away from the city really want to stay in Sawtown, Arkansas? I don't know. But, in the end, it's your decision, honey. You'll have done a bit more than your agreed obligation by finding another doctor."

"Matthew said he won't be back until I can tell him I've broken up with Ryan."

"That shows his sense of ethics, Emily. It explains why I didn't see him in the Blue Bird today, too. He's probably gone out to the cutting area for awhile. He said once that when he's upset about something he goes into the trees for comfort."

Emily set her glass down on the table with a bang. "Well, if cutting down trees gives him comfort, I think he can just stay there."

"I don't believe he was talking about cutting them down, Emily. I hope he comes in soon. You and he need to talk."

"We did talk, Mom," Emily answered tiredly. "I think he's said all he wants to say to me."

Caroline looked at Emily with tender understanding. "I need to do some things inside, honey. But stay and finish your coffee." She leaned forward and kissed Emily lightly on the forehead before she gathered up her own plate and glass and went inside.

Emily smiled to herself in spite of her distress. For as long as she could remember, her mom had left her alone on the patio whenever she was upset. A few times Caroline had even bundled her up in heavy clothes and let her sit out there and watch it snow.

She sat there for a long time, but she didn't feel the comfort that Caroline had wanted for her. Finally she went around the house to her car. She knew that her mother wouldn't be upset that she didn't say good-bye.

❧

"Emily," Dr. Anderson's voice on the phone was tight with tension, "I'm afraid I don't have as good of news about Mrs. Adams as I did for Mrs. Logan."

Emily slowly rearranged a few papers on her desk before she forced herself to ask the question her colleague waited for. "It's malignant?"

"It is. I'm sorry, Emily. I know she's an old friend." Dr. Anderson's voice echoed the feeling in his words.

"What is the prognosis you see now?" Emily hoped the tears she was forcing back didn't sound in her own voice. This news, added to the week of indecision and loneliness of not hearing from either Matthew or Ryan (or God, she thought sadly), was devastating. Then she forced her thoughts away from herself and toward Angeline as she listened to his answer.

"That's as close as we can come to good news. We did a modified mastectomy and she's agreed to start chemotherapy. When I discharge her she can come in to your clinic for the chemo and won't have to drive into Clinton. I can't tell you how much you're doing for Sawtown, Emily, just being there. And, barring any setbacks, the prognosis should be good. You know, we doctors don't ever promise a complete cure, but we can try for that when we find the cancer early enough. I think, in this case, in particular because of her attitude, we'll get one."

"Great." Emily tried to make her voice match her words. "Tell her I'll drive in to see her late this afternoon."

"I'll do that. I'll try to be around, Emily."

Emily thanked him and hung up to go find Kate where she was working in one of the examination rooms. Kate's reaction was optimistic. "Emily, we can just thank God you're here and had the idea to do these mammograms," she said, stopping momentarily in the act of replacing supplies. "You may have saved a life that's badly needed here. Now we'll just try to get the clinic cleared out so you can leave early. You're looking a little, to use a hotshot professional term, pale around the gills lately. Was Saturday too much for you? Are you sure you're sleeping enough?"

Emily managed a smile. "No, Mother. Yes, Mother. At

least I'm sleeping fairly well," she added honestly.

"Well, whatever it is that's keeping Matthew hermiting in the woods and you looking like somebody declared war on you, it's not that he fell for Dr. Blake. Al and I know that and you should too." Kate hesitated. "I'm sorry, Emily, I don't mean to interfere."

Emily touched her lightly on the shoulder. "It's okay, Kate. And I do know that he didn't fall for Joyce."

Cammie came in then to tell them that the waiting room was filling up. "Well, if we're going to get you away to Clifton early, we'd better get cracking," Kate said, closing the last cabinet door with finality.

"As if that ever will happen on a Friday afternoon, especially just before school starts," Emily said pessimistically.

⁂

It was evening before she got in to the Clifton hospital. She found Reverend Adams at his wife's bedside. Angeline Adams was drowsy, but fully aware of the results of the surgery. She caught Emily's hand.

"I'd hug you but I'm a little sore just now," she joked. "But, Emily, I do have to tell you, Ethan and I have always been proud of you, even when you were a little girl, but we didn't realize that you would grow up to save my life. And I do expect to live a long time after this. But if you hadn't been there—if you hadn't got us all in for mammograms— I kept saying I was going to go in for a mammogram like all the good advice-givers said I should, but I was always just too busy."

Her voice drifted off as she drowsed, but her words were reflected in the grateful tears in Reverend Adams' eyes.

"I know God doesn't lay more on us than we can bear,

but I don't see how I could do my job as well without her. Emily, can I tell you how often I've thanked Him for you today?"

Driving home, Emily rolled her window down and let the soft night air flow smoothly over her face. "God," she whispered, "is this Your answer to me?"

At home she found a letter from Joyce. She almost decided to let it wait till morning so she could sit down with a cup of cappuccino and have a long discussion with herself without any intrusion from outside. She ground the coffee and started the machine.

While the coffee maker purred, she found her finger running under the flap of the envelope. Sighing, she opened it and pulled out the heavy sheet of faintly rose-colored paper, smiling in spite of herself at the elegant monogram at the top.

She leaned against the kitchen counter and started to quickly scan the letter.

> *Dear Emily,*
>   *Thank you for having me down and letting me see Sawtown and Arkansas. And I was right about one thing. Nobody here believes that I went diamond mining. Tell Matthew that even my pretty rock doesn't convince them. And thanks to Caroline and Ben for the lovely barbecue. I loved meeting them and greatly admire their obvious contentment with the life they're making for themselves. I do understand why someone who grew up in that beautiful country would*

*insist that you not only can, but must, go
home again.*

*Now, Emily, I have to be honest with you
to give you time to look for another doctor if
you still want to go to Ryan in Africa.
Though I can't imagine why you would
choose Africa (or Ryan, handsome as he is)
with that great guy right there who is so
obviously in love with you.*

Emily sank down into a chair and leaned her elbows on
the kitchen table, letting her head sink against her hands
for a minute. "I'm not sure I'm ready for this," she whispered.

*Anyway, I've given this a lot of sober
thought since I visited you there and I've
decided it's time to be honest with myself as
well as you. My desire to get away from the
city and my parents' lifestyle was pure
romanticism. Much as I enjoyed seeing you
again and meeting your friends and your
mom, well, I'll put it bluntly. . .home looked
good to me. I haven't decided yet if I'm
going to change my specialty, but I'm going
to stay here, Emily. And visit you sometimes,
if you still want me to.*

*I can't tell you how sorry I am for telling
Matthew about your plans. I can only hope it
will be, or was, a springboard to a searching
of both your hearts. Because even from way
outside, I can see what is truly in both your*

>*hearts. And I did mean to repeat* both *your*
>*hearts. Don't let it get lost, Emily. Didn't St.*
>*Paul have a lot to say about the importance*
>*of love in the world?*
>   *Will close before I get too sentimental.*
>   *Still love you,*
>   *Joyce*

Emily put the letter down on the table. Without letting herself put the emotions churning through her mind into words, she went to the coffee maker and drained some into her mug and added a hot froth of milk. This time she didn't bother with chocolate.

She carried it into the living room and sat down on the same place on her couch where she had sat during her last conversation with Matthew. She swallowed several sips of the rich beverage before she accepted the simple truth.

"Answer number two, isn't it, God? I don't even have to worry about hurting Ryan. Every one of his letters tells me that he has more in common with that unnamed nurse than with me.

"I only have to think about seeing Matthew and I ache to see him. It's been five days since he went back into the forest.

"Tomorrow, when we close the clinic for Saturday afternoon, I'll go find him and tell him I love him. Now, it's only fair to tell Ryan that I'm freeing him. And me.

"Thank You, God."

She found it easier than she could have imagined to write Ryan a long, affectionate, but honest letter.

fourteen

"Kate, can you take my beeper this afternoon? Call Dr. Anderson for advice if you get anything you don't want to handle."

Kate looked up from the Saturday morning charts she was finishing, a happy smile beginning to draw her lips upward. Cammie was already gone after a slow Saturday morning.

"Of course, Emily. I'm just going to work in my garden this afternoon, so it won't be a problem." She hesitated, then seemed unable to keep from asking, "Does this mean that Matthew has come out of his retreat? Even the sawyers who've come into the Blue Bird say they haven't seen him this week."

Emily shook her head. "He hasn't come back." She was tempted to tell Kate that she was going after him but something held her back. Maybe the fear that Kate would insist on getting Al or Ben to go with her. She didn't want any company on this trip.

Emily had lived too long on the forest's edge to have romantic ideas about the ease of walking into it. She layered light to heavy shirts over blue jeans and pulled on high-topped boots over thick socks. She'd seen too many snakes to panic at the sight of one, but she intended to protect herself as much as possible. She sprayed herself liberally with insect repellent and put the can in her back-pack.

She put a couple of sandwiches and a long flashlight in the backpack and turned her car in the direction of Caroline's house. But she went past the turnoff to the lane down to her mother's home. It wasn't Caroline that she wanted to talk to this afternoon.

She remembered that the lumber road where the logs and boards were brought out of the decimated forest was just beyond Caroline's lane, and she slowed down on the empty highway to watch for it.

The road leading back through second growth timber looked dimmer than she remembered and she hoped that meant that Matthew was bringing out a few less trees. She slowed almost to a stop to turn onto it.

She was soon bouncing over rocks and into potholes that were covered from her sight by a generous growth of mixed vegetation. Yet tracks showed that a vehicle had come through here recently. Was it Matthew's Jeep? She kept following them.

The farther she got into the forest, the closer the young trees seemed to skim the sides of her car, as though the forest was quietly and determinedly taking back its territory, tree by tree.

It was becoming obvious that the road was no longer in use. Beginning to feel a flash of apprehension, she drove on.

Soon she admitted that she was on the wrong road and started looking for a place where she dared to pull far enough out of the tracks she was following to turn around.

Trying to back several miles between trees didn't appeal to her, and the hope of coming onto Matthew's Jeep kept surfacing within her.

Did he have a place back here? A camping area? A cabin? There must be something because, though she'd overheard several people mentioning that he hadn't come into town or been seen at the cutting area, no one seemed concerned about him.

She came around a slight bend to see a small tree growing defiantly in the center of the road. Tire tracks and partially flattened vegetation showed that Matthew—she was convinced now that it was Matthew—had pulled out around it. She followed, now so sure that it was his Jeep she was trailing that she no longer thought of turning around.

She heard a sudden, sharp, clang under the car and felt a shudder. The engine died. Guessing that she had hit a rock hidden under the long grass, she turned the ignition key off and gave herself a few minutes to stop shaking before she tried it again. It caught and she put the car in reverse to back off the rock and attempt to go around it even if she had to go out of Matthew's tracks.

There was a tearing screech under the car as something broke. The engine stopped again and Emily didn't try to restart it. Whatever the rock had done had been disastrous.

She forced herself to take some kind of sensible stock of her situation. She was alone and on her own. Matthew might not come by for days, and no one knew where she had planned to go. If she wanted out of here, she was going to have to walk.

She put the car keys in her pocket and stepped out into

the high grass. She strapped the backpack on and took the few steps to the road and stood there in indecision. A glance at the sun told her that it was already well past mid-afternoon. She couldn't walk back to the highway and to Caroline's house before dark.

And the tire tracks went on. Matthew had to be in there. Maybe she was only a short distance from him. She might be driving out with him in less than an hour. If she didn't find him, the idea of spending a night alone in the woods didn't appeal to her, but it didn't make her panic.

Without giving the road back another glance, she took off, walking in one tire track, in the direction that she hoped would lead her to Matthew. She lengthened her stride as much as she could, flailing at the cloud of tiny gnats that seemed to have been waiting for a chance to fly as close as possible to her face and ears, in spite of her earlier application of repellent.

She considered, as though it were a weighty question, whether to take the trouble to stop and dig the can of repellent out of her backpack or endure the gnats. Without making a conscious decision, she trudged on.

Two hours later, she stopped at the bottom of one of an ever higher series of hills and leaned against a tree, puffing strenuously. She had thought she was still in good condition from years of walking down long hospital corridors, but walking in light shoes down straight smooth floors was nothing like dragging heavy boots across overgrown hills.

In spite of the dimness of the forest, she was hot in her heavy shirt. She thought of taking it off, slapped a mosquito, and changed her mind. This time, she dug her repellent out of her backpack and sprayed herself again. *At least,* she thought wryly, *Matthew can never accuse me of enticing him with my perfume.*

After resting a few minutes, she forced her tired legs to stumble up the hill.

At the top, she was suddenly in another world. The unexpected glare of the late sun glittered across an ugly scene. The whole side of a sharply rising hill had been clear cut of old growth as far as she could see. "Oh, Matthew," she whispered, looking at it in dismay, "how could you?"

But nestled into a small cut in the hill, beside a huge fallen tree, was a small cabin. Matthew must be here.

Her legs suddenly garnered new life and she actually found herself able to hurry up the tire tracks that seemed to go around the cabin, though she couldn't see the Jeep.

She kept her eyes on the cabin. It was a simple square, and she knew before she reached it that it would be one room with a rough cot and a camp stove and plank table serving for a kitchen. But it didn't matter. It wouldn't take long to tell Matthew that she had written Ryan that she wouldn't be coming to Africa.

She knocked on the handleless door and waited. There was no answer and no sound from inside. After knocking again she gave the door a slight push. It opened easily. The cabin was empty.

The room looked exactly as she had pictured it except for one thing. In her thoughts, she had seen Matthew coming toward her, his eyes showing his happiness that she had cared enough to come looking for him and tell him what he wanted to hear.

Disappointment was a sharp wave of pain. Then she had a moment of fear. Was it really Matthew she had followed up here to this scarred and empty section of the forest? Should she turn around and try to get back to some kind of civilization and safety before dark?

She stood, indecisively, in the doorway for several minutes. The silence was as absolute as though no one had been in the cabin for years, but a faint odor of bacon told her that someone had prepared and eaten a meal not too long ago.

She decided to at least look around before running. Maybe she could find some hint of the person who had occupied the hut so recently.

There were no cupboards or even any shelves. A skillet and a battered old tin coffee pot were the only two kitchen utensils, and they both sat on a table nailed up from rough slabs of wood. Whoever lived here apparently ate out of the skillet, for she couldn't see any plates. A half empty plastic sack of paper cups lying by the skillet looked like a rocket ship put into an 1880s movie set. One lone fork lay beside it. A large cooler on the floor proved to be empty and dried. A memory of such a cooler floating down Cricket Creek made her hope that it might be Matthew's. But both the cooler here and the one on the float creek were so ordinary that they could have belonged to anyone.

"Well, I'm finding out a lot about Mr. Whoever just like Sherlock Holmes." She tried to force thoughts into her mind to keep from crying. "He doesn't use sugar unless he stirs it in with a fork and he didn't leave any food here, so he apparently doesn't plan to return soon. At least I won't have to worry about someone coming in on me."

The thought itself made her realize that she would have to stay till morning. It would certainly be better than trying to push her exhausted legs back to the highway.

She went to the narrow cot, wondering how dirty the sheet might be, if there was a sheet. It looked like there was barely a mattress. A rough wool blanket was spread haphazardly over it. She lifted it up and forgot to look at the sheet.

A pocket knife fell out of the folds, hitting the floor with a sharp clang. Grinning suddenly, she picked it up and clasped it in both hands. The multipurpose woodsman's knife was Matthew's. It was the one he had used to cut sticks for the fire he had built for Julie on the canoe trip. She didn't need to see his initials on the side to know it was his, but she found them fascinating and rubbed her fingers over them slowly.

"Oh," she breathed, "I wish I could hug you, little knife. But look at me, talking to a knife. No, I feel like I'm talking to Matthew, even though he's taken everything and—what?—gone back to town or somewhere farther back in the woods? Well, never mind, now I feel comfortable staying here tonight."

She realized suddenly how hungry she was. She got out her sandwiches and the bottle of water and started to sit down on the rough bench at the table. Then she felt a sudden desire to be outside again. Holding the comforting knife cradled in the palm of her hand, she went out.

The huge tree on the ground beside the end of the hut looked like it had been left just as it had fallen years ago from a now nearly rotted stump. It was old and half rotten, and though Emily was sure she'd soon be covered with curious or hungry bugs from inside it, she felt a strong inner urge to sit on it. Later. Now she walked the length of it, wondering what it was about it that caught her attention. Something wasn't right. Something. . .

The answer came to her slowly. The big end of the tree had been sawed almost through but it had been left just as it fell. Even the once sharp shards of wood it had torn from itself when it fell were lying across the stump. And the black limbs that had survived the years were still on it.

It shouldn't have been cut and then left to rot. It should have been dressed and taken out to sell. There would have been many board feet of lumber in it. Why had this one tree not been treated like all the others?

Could it be? She had never been back to the place where her father had been crushed by a tree that had been left just as it fell. Never dressed. Never sent to market.

Tears filled her eyes. Was she standing where her father had died? She whirled around with her back to the tree, shutting the thought out. She could get used to it slowly. After awhile, she turned back and walked along its length again.

There was life. The dead tree was nourishing and sheltering life everywhere. Big and little ants, as well as other insects, ran along its trunk. Several Monarch butterflies landed on wildflowers growing about the trunk and took off again, probably with migration on their minds.

A tiny chipmunk ran out of the branches and stopped a short distance away to look at her. She caught a glimpse of brown and white among the branches and wondered if she had been given a rare look at a sleeping whippoorwill. She could see, under the trunk, a bigger hole that had been dug out and that probably sheltered a fox and her babies.

She deliberately recalled the few memories she had of her father and the way Caroline had said he loved the forest. If this was the tree that killed him, he would be more pleased with this monument than with the dead stone that marked his grave in the church cemetery.

She knelt and gently blew several tiny ants off the trunk, then sat down. Inside her she felt the sharp-edged pain that had been there since childhood begin to soften.

Still holding her sandwiches and water but forgetting her earlier hunger and thirst, she sat looking about her in the early dusk. Finally she let her gaze rest on the decimated hillside in front of her. She straightened with surprise.

Now that the sun's glare had given way to a soft evening light, she could see tiny trees scattered about the clear cut area. And she knew Matthew was doing what he said he wanted to do. He had come in to the area that Morgan Lumbar had continued to clear cut right up to the time he'd bought the company, cleared out the trash bushes that grew up, and replanted it in trees.

It would be years before the scars on the land were gone, but two scars in herself had been smoothed away here in this lonely cabin. Yet it was no longer really lonely, for something of Matthew was there with her, wherever he may have gone.

A shadowy shape came out of the far trees and bounded across the hill toward her.

"Boone?" she called, "how did you find me?"

The dog came up to her confidently. He acted as if he were home, and Emily realized that the den under the tree trunk must be his. Laughing without asking herself why, Emily pulled off hunks of her sandwiches and shared them with the dog. Then she poured a bit of water into the palm of her hand and he licked it off.

When it was fully dark, Emily went in and, without using her flashlight, found the cot and laid down in her clothes. Just before she slid into a sound sleep, she heard Boone bumping himself down against the unlatched door with a deep sigh.

She was wakened by the sound of Boone growling. Then she heard voices. No, the one voice in the world she wanted to hear. Matthew, trying to wheedle his way past the dog.

"Come on, Boone. I'm her friend. Good dog. Good friend. She'll vouch for me if you just let me by."

It was still dark, but Emily felt no indecision about where she was. Laughing to herself, she fumbled on the floor to where she had left the flashlight, found it, and switched it on.

"Matthew?" she called, shuffling her boots across the floor with legs that felt like they had run the Boston marathon twice. She caught the edge of the door in her fingers and pulled it inward. "Matthew. You came."

Matthew stood in the glare of his headlights. "See, Boone, I told you she'd vouch for me. Now if you'll just move and turn your head, I'm going to kiss her."

Obligingly, Boone moved away. Matthew stood for a minute looking at her in the combined glow of the flashlight and his Jeep lights. Then he took one step forward and kept his promise to Boone quite thoroughly. Emily didn't try to tell herself that it was her Boston Marathon legs that made her feel weak and light-headed as she wholeheartedly joined in the kiss.

Then she drew away as far as his arms would allow. "I thought you weren't going to do that again until—"

Another kiss stopped her as he lifted her off the floor to the level of his lips. Without putting her down or moving his mouth very far from hers he answered, "I talked to your mom this afternoon when I was trying to find you. She said you were wavering, so it occurred to me that I might help you make a decision. Then when I finally found Kate and she said you went off on some secret mission, I guessed. . .hoped. . .what it was."

"I was trying to find you, but you weren't here and my car got stuck—something broke I think—trying to follow your Jeep tracks and then I walked a million miles and Boone came for supper and we went to sleep."

"I know. I finally figured where you might have gone and that we must have just missed each other. I went out down the other lumber road, the one that's still open to the mill. When no one had seen you there, I was on my way back to town when I remembered that you hadn't seen these roads for years and you might not know that nobody but me uses this one anymore. When I saw your car and you weren't anywhere near it, I nearly died. I made God enough promises on the way up here to keep me busy the rest of my life."

"Matthew, does it mean something that we both decided to go find each other at the same time?"

"It means I love you and I hope you love me and we're ideally suited to each other."

Emily looked up at him. "I love you, Matthew," she said simply and honestly.

He grabbed her up and kissed her again. "I'm making up for lost time," he crowed.

Emily laughed. "Speaking of time, what time is it?"

"Only about eleven, sleepyhead. Time goes fast when you go to sleep at dark." Slowly, reluctantly, he put her down. "I've got a thermos in the Jeep. Want some coffee before we go back to town or go to the Blue Bird and have something with it?"

"At the Blue Bird, please. Boone ate most of my sandwiches. And I have a lot to tell you about the little trees I saw that you planted and I know you're really trying to take care of the forest and I finally turned my father loose tonight and. . ."

"Whoa, sweetheart, we have the rest of our lives to talk."

"And, if God chooses, we'll spend them right here in Sawtown where we're both needed."

"By choice, but anywhere so long as we're together," Matthew said, kissing her one last time before they closed the door and went to his Jeep.

Just before he started it up, Boone took a sudden flying leap and landed with a grunt in the back seat. Then he sat up and tried hard to look like he had been riding there all his life.

Matthew and Emily looked at each other and burst into loud whoops of happy laughter that echoed across the barren hill, throwing out a promise of life coming back to a place that would one day be beautiful again.

A Letter To Our Readers

Dear Reader:

In order that we might better contribute to your reading enjoyment, we would appreciate your taking a few minutes to respond to the following questions. When completed, please return to the following:

Rebecca Germany, Editor
Heartsong Presents
P.O. Box 719
Uhrichsville, Ohio 44683

1. Did you enjoy reading *A Place for Love*?
   - ❏ Very much. I would like to see more books by this author!
   - ❏ Moderately
     I would have enjoyed it more if _____

     _____

2. Are you a member of **Heartsong Presents**? ❏Yes ❏No
   If no, where did you purchase this book?_____

   _____

3. What influenced your decision to purchase this book? (Check those that apply.)

   - ❏ Cover
   - ❏ Back cover copy
   - ❏ Title
   - ❏ Friends
   - ❏ Publicity
   - ❏ Other_____

4. How would you rate, on a scale from 1 (poor) to 5 (superior), **Heartsong Presents'** new cover design?_____

5. On a scale from 1 (poor) to 10 (superior), please rate the following elements.

    ___Heroine   ___Plot

    ___Hero   ___Inspirational theme

    ___Setting   ___Secondary characters

6. What settings would you like to see covered in **Heartsong Presents** books?_____

    _____

    _____

7. What are some inspirational themes you would like to see treated in future books?_____

    _____

    _____

8. Would you be interested in reading other **Heartsong Presents** titles?   ❑ Yes   ❑ No

9. Please check your age range:
    ❑ Under 18   ❑ 18-24   ❑ 25-34
    ❑ 35-45   ❑ 46-55   ❑ Over 55

10. How many hours per week do you read? _____

Name _____

Occupation _____

Address _____

City_____ State_____ Zip_____

Don't miss these favorite Heartsong Presents *titles by some of our most distinguished authors!*

(*Voted favorites by our readers in a recent poll.*)

Your price is only $2.95 each!

___HP59 EYES OF THE HEART, *Maryn Langer*
___HP62 THE WILLING HEART, *Janelle Jamison*
___HP66 AUTUMN LOVE, *Ann Bell**
___HP70 A NEW SONG, *Kathleen Yapp**
___HP76 HEARTBREAK TRAIL, *VeraLee Wiggins*
___HP78 A SIGN OF LOVE, *Veda Boyd Jones**
___HP81 BETTER THAN FRIENDS, *Sally Laity**
___HP82 SOUTHERN GENTLEMAN, *Yvonne Lehman**
___HP83 MARTHA MY OWN, *VeraLee Wiggins*
___HP84 HEART'S DESIRE, *Paige Winship Dooley*
___HP85 LAMP IN DARKNESS, *Connie Loraine**
___HP86 POCKETFUL OF LOVE, *Loree Lough**
___HP87 SIGN OF THE BOW, *Kay Cornelius*
___HP88 BEYOND TODAY, *Janelle Jamison*
___HP90 CATER TO A WHIM, *Norma Jean Lutz**
___HP92 ABRAM MY LOVE, *VeraLee Wiggins*

*contemporary title

Heart♥ng

Any 12
Heartsong
Presents titles
for only
$26.95 **

CONTEMPORARY ROMANCE IS CHEAPER BY THE DOZEN!

Buy any assortment of twelve *Heartsong Presents* titles and save 25% off of the already discounted price of $2.95 each!

**plus $1.00 shipping and handling per order and sales tax where applicable.

HEARTSONG PRESENTS TITLES AVAILABLE NOW:

_HP 3 RESTORE THE JOY, *Sara Mitchell*
_HP 4 REFLECTIONS OF THE HEART, *Sally Laity**
_HP 5 THIS TREMBLING CUP, *Marlene Chase*
_HP 6 THE OTHER SIDE OF SILENCE, *Marlene Chase*
_HP 9 HEARTSTRINGS, *Irene B. Brand**
_HP 10 SONG OF LAUGHTER, *Lauraine Snelling**
_HP 13 PASSAGE OF THE HEART, *Kjersti Hoff Baez*
_HP 14 A MATTER OF CHOICE, *Susannah Hayden*
_HP 18 LLAMA LADY, *VeraLee Wiggins**
_HP 19 ESCORT HOMEWARD, *Eileen M. Berger**
_HP 21 GENTLE PERSUASION, *Veda Boyd Jones*
_HP 22 INDY GIRL, *Brenda Bancroft*
_HP 25 REBAR, *Mary Carpenter Reid*
_HP 26 MOUNTAIN HOUSE, *Mary Louise Colln*
_HP 29 FROM THE HEART, *Sara Mitchell*
_HP 30 A LOVE MEANT TO BE, *Brenda Bancroft*
_HP 33 SWEET SHELTER, *VeraLee Wiggins*
_HP 34 UNDER A TEXAS SKY, *Veda Boyd Jones*
_HP 37 DRUMS OF SHELOMOH, *Yvonne Lehman*
_HP 38 A PLACE TO CALL HOME, *Eileen M. Berger*
_HP 41 FIELDS OF SWEET CONTENT, *Norma Jean Lutz*
_HP 42 SEARCH FOR TOMORROW, *Mary Hawkins*
_HP 45 DESIGN FOR LOVE, *Janet Gortsema*
_HP 46 THE GOVERNOR'S DAUGHTER, *Veda Boyd Jones*
_HP 49 YESTERDAY'S TOMORROWS, *Linda Herring*
_HP 50 DANCE IN THE DISTANCE, *Kjersti Hoff Baez*
_HP 53 MIDNIGHT MUSIC, *Janelle Burnham*
_HP 54 HOME TO HER HEART, *Lena Nelson Dooley*
_HP 57 LOVE'S SILKEN MELODY, *Norma Jean Lutz*
_HP 58 FREE TO LOVE, *Doris English*
_HP 61 PICTURE PERFECT, *Susan Kirby*
_HP 62 A REAL AND PRECIOUS THING, *Brenda Bancroft*
_HP 65 ANGEL FACE, *Frances Carfi Matranga*
_HP 66 AUTUMN LOVE, *Ann Bell*
_HP 69 BETWEEN LOVE AND LOYALTY, *Susannah Hayden*
_HP 70 A NEW SONG, *Kathleen Yapp*
_HP 73 MIDSUMMER'S DREAM, *Rena Eastman*
_HP 74 SANTANONI SUNRISE, *Hope Irvin Marston and Claire M. Coughlin*

*Temporarily out of stock.

(If ordering from this page, please remember to include it with the order form.)

Presents

Great Inspirational Romance at a Great Price!

Heartsong Presents books are inspirational romances in contemporary and historical settings, designed to give you an enjoyable, spirit-lifting reading experience. You can choose from 144 wonderfully written titles from some of today's best authors like Colleen L. Reece, Brenda Bancroft, Janelle Jamison, and many others.

When ordering quantities less than twelve, above titles are $2.95 each.

SEND TO: Heartsong Presents Reader's Service
P.O. Box 719, Uhrichsville, Ohio 44683

Please send me the items checked above. I am enclosing $_____
(please add $1.00 to cover postage per order. OH add 6.25% tax. NJ add 6%.). Send check or money order, no cash or C.O.D.s, please.
To place a credit card order, call 1-800-847-8270.

NAME _____

ADDRESS _____

CITY/STATE _____ ZIP _____

Heart♥ng Presents
Love Stories Are Rated G!

That's for godly, gratifying, and of course, great! If you love a thrilling love story, but don't appreciate the sordidness of popular paperback romances, **Heartsong Presents** is for you. In fact, **Heartsong Presents** is the *only inspirational romance book club*, the only one featuring love stories where Christian faith is the primary ingredient in a marriage relationship.

Sign up today to receive your first set of four, never before published Christian romances. Send no money now; you will receive a bill with the first shipment. You may cancel at any time without obligation, and if you aren't completely satisfied with any selection, you may return the books for an immediate refund!

Imagine. . .four new romances every four weeks—two historical, two contemporary—with men and women like you who long to meet the one God has chosen as the love of their lives. . .all for the low price of $9.97 postpaid.

To join, simply complete the coupon below and mail to the address provided. **Heartsong Presents** romances are rated G for another reason: They'll arrive *Godspeed!*

YES! Sign me up for Heart♥ng!

NEW MEMBERSHIPS WILL BE SHIPPED IMMEDIATELY!
Send no money now. We'll bill you only $9.97 post-paid with your first shipment of four books. Or for faster action, call toll free 1-800-847-8270.

NAME _____

ADDRESS _____

CITY _____ STATE _____ ZIP _____

MAIL TO: HEARTSONG PRESENTS, P.O. Box 719, Uhrichsville, Ohio 44683

YES 8-95